TO BE THE BEST
Book One: Six Minutes

BY H.L. HERTEL

HH Castle-Mac Publishing
Saint Louis Park, MN

ISBN: 978-0-615-21892-2

Published by HH Castle-Mac Publishing, St Louis Park, MN. Printed by Lightning Source.

Books published by HH Castle-Mac Publishing are available at quantity discounts on bulk purchases for premium, education, fund-raising and special sales use. For details, please write to: SALES DEPARTMENT, HH CASTLE-MAC PUBLISHING, P.O. BOX 16513, ST LOUIS PARK, MN 55416-0513.

Dedication

For Kathleen and Melbourne, my loving parents, who always loved and supported me and would have done so even if (hypothetically speaking, of course) I would have arrived home from a wrestling tournament at 3:00 a.m. with a broken nose stuffed full of cotton.

Acknowledgements

Thank you so much to my wonderful wife Lisa who has worn many hats in this process (editor and sounding board to name two) and has given me such amazing support in bringing this story to life. Also, extra-special thanks to my sister Heidi and brother-in-law Brian for their input on the current wrestling environment which enabled me to make some key adjustments. Finally, thank you to my sister Darci and final-round test-readers Jordan, John, Carol and Dan whose input has strengthened the final product.

Introduction

When I first started writing this book in the fall of 1994, I had no idea what twists and turns the writing process (not to mention my life in general) would take. After about five years, I realized that the entire story was too long for one novel and so I found a natural breaking point and separated it into two parts. The first part was finally completed and copyrighted in November 2003 as a screenplay entitled *Six Minutes*. After getting positive feedback from a few dozen friends, family members and others, I received a professional opinion that "Getting a screen play made into a movie is like carrying a refrigerator up a mountain" but that the story was enjoyable and unique enough to try as a book. I then embarked on the task of converting the screenplay into a novel.

What you are about to read is the result of converting that screenplay. It is a story that stands on its own but, in my mind, is still unfinished. Thanks to the wonderful response from readers of this first installment, I have begun the process of finalizing the sequel novel. Updates regarding its projected completion date and availability will be posted on the publisher's website, www.HHCastle-Mac.com, beginning in 2010.

Prologue

The two wrestlers faced each other, neither blinked. This was the championship match. While both boys felt un-beatable, only one would prove himself to be so tonight.

William Castle sat in the bleachers and relished the contest. Wrestling was his first love and still held a special place in his heart, despite the fact that it had fallen to number three on his 'love list'. Yes, a wife and family had taken the top two spots. He glanced down at his boys, Ron and Nick, sitting to either side of him. It was heartwarming to see them both completely mesmerized by the event.

The wrestler in green was the first to make his move. He shot in on his opponent's legs, his quickness catching the boy in red off guard. As the boy in red scrambled to his stomach, his opponent took a position of control. The referee held up two fingers exclaiming, "Takedown, two points green."

William was glad to see that the referee had given the green ankle-band to the wrestler in green and the red band to his opponent. This would make it easier for William's boys to follow the match as he attempted to describe the sport's basic rules.

"You see, once he takes him to the mat, gets behind him and has control, that is a takedown. He gets two points," William instructed.

The boys, both with mouths hanging open, nodded without taking their eyes off the match.

William had to smile. He wasn't surprised to see eight-year-old Ron so interested. The boy was a bit of a terror and was probably watching the match more to find ideas for playground fights than he was to learn a new form of competition. Ron's jet-black hair was a genetic gift from his mother but William would be hard-pressed to name the ancestor responsible for the boy's wild, aggressive personality.

Aggression was paying off for the wrestler in green. He managed to turn his opponent to his back and was holding him there as the referee watched closely. At this point, all it would take was for red's shoulder blades to touch the mat for an instant. That would be a pin and the match would be over. After eight seconds on his back, the red wrestler was able to return to his stomach and temporary safety.

"Near fall, three points green," bellowed the ref.

William felt the familiar tug on his left hand. He glanced down at Nick, whose curiosity allowed him to briefly break his stare and whisper, "Daddy, what was that?"

Squeezing the boy's hand, William explained, loud enough for Ron to hear as well, that a 'near fall' was also known as 'back points'. It was a reward, in the form of two or three points, which was given to a wrestler who holds his opponent's back to the mat but does not succeed in pinning him.

Nick squeezed his dad's hand and smiled before turning back to the match. Yes, this was William's six-and-a-half-year-old cozy boy. Dressed in a *Star Wars* sweatshirt, he was much more comfortable playing with toys than he was getting scuffed in physical competition. His scratches and bruises were less from his own adventures than from his older brother's regular tormenting. His light-brown hair was similar to what was left of William's own.

As time ticked down on the first two-minute period, the red wrestler on the bottom scrambled to his feet, broke green's grip and faced his opponent, earning him an escape. The referee signaled for a point, "Escape, one point red."

Four seconds later, a foghorn sounded, ending the period.

"That was a fast two minutes," thought William. He remembered his high school matches. Those three periods totaled only six minutes but could feel like a week.

The referee flipped a red and green coin. It came up green, giving the choice of starting position for the second period to the green wrestler. The boy looked at his corner and, after receiving a signal from his coach, opted to defer his decision until the third period. The boy in red was then given the choice and chose 'down'.

"Of course," thought William. To less experienced onlookers, choosing to start a period on the bottom seemed like a vulnerable position. However, to many wrestlers, this was like getting a free point as it is often easier to escape from an opponent than to hold an opponent down.

Upon the referee's direction, "Bottom man set," red got down on his hands and knees in the middle of the mat. Green circled behind him and received the signal, "Top man on." Green grabbed red's left elbow with one hand and put his other arm around red's waist.

The quiet murmur of the crowd filled the gym before the referee signaled, "Ready…wrestle."

The two boys lunged forward with red trying to get away and green trying to turn red to his back. In the impending flurry, green made a mistake, lost control and found himself on the bottom with red taking control of him.

The referee's exclamation, "Reversal, two points red," was lost to most as many fans got excited, yelling and cheering for red. The referee signaled for two points.

Again, William felt the tug on his left hand and heard his younger son's voice.

"Daddy, what was that?"

"That was a reversal, Nicky. When he's on the bottom and turns things around so that he's on top, he gets two points."

Nick nodded in satisfaction, "A reversal, I know that."

"No you don't!" Ron was able to tear his attention away from the match long enough to argue with his brother.

"Yes I do!"

William intervened, "Stop it you two! Watch the match."

"Do not!" Ron continued.

"Ron!" His father's tone was enough to quiet the boy.

The brothers glared at each other for a moment before turning their attention back to the match.

* * *

An hour later, the tournament was over. The wrestlers took their turns moving proudly to the awards stand, getting their medals and getting their pictures taken. William's memories drifted back to his high school days, standing tall on the platform in several tournaments. He had led the boys down to the mat for a closer view of the ceremony.

"Daddy?"

"Yes Nick."

The boy made a few clumsy moves against an invisible opponent, which vaguely resembled some takedowns he had witnessed. "When I grow up, I'm going to be the best wrestler there is."

Not to be outdone, his brother piped in, "No, I'm gonna be the best!"

"Why did this always have to be such a contest?" William thought.

"Ron, stop hassling your little brother. There are lots of weight classes. You can both be the best."

Ron glared quickly at his brother with big brown eyes. He was quite fluid as he too pretended to wrestle an opponent. Under his breath he whispered, "I'm gonna be the best."

He then turned and stared intensely at the boys on the podium as a man in a suit handed the gold medal to the boy on the top step. "I'm gonna be the best," he repeated softly. The look in his eyes would make any adult hesitate to doubt him.

Chapter 1

A whistle split the air.

"Stalemate!" The referee's voice was loud and squeaky. "Neither man able to improve his position."

"There are probably a lot of people watching who don't know what a stalemate is," thought Ron. It would stand to reason that many people who don't even care about wrestling would pay attention to the state high school championships. For all he knew, the entire world was watching the title match of the 125-pound weight class.

An instant later, Ron allowed himself to fall back into a sitting position on the mat, releasing his opponent, Tony Simms. Tony was clearly exhausted; his chest heaved as he looked back at Ron. He looked like he would soon be ill.

"This is good," thought Ron. All year, he had used a three-tiered system. First, he would try to beat his opponent based on pure technique. This worked in about three-quarters of his matches. Unfortunately, Simms was a tough competitor and had come out aggressive, quickly scoring points on Ron and forcing him to adjust to his back-up plan – winning on conditioning. Ron had wrestled in such a way during the second period that it had forced both boys to use a lot of energy. His superior conditioning was now paying off, which was fortunate as he did not want to have to try to out-muscle Simms, Ron's option of last resort.

With his wet, black hair plastered to his forehead, Ron raced quickly back to the center of the mat. He had some concern that his opponent's last elbow had been too well placed. He noticed the copper-like taste in his mouth and knew that the blood would soon begin flowing from his nostril.

"HURRY UP!" Ron's thoughts were intense as Simms sluggishly crawled to the center of the mat and assumed the bottom referee's position.

"Top man on," the referee beckoned.

As Ron hurriedly followed directions, the referee noticed the blood appearing below his right nostril.

"Injury time out red," he bellowed.

"I'm all right!" Ron exclaimed, not wanting to relinquish his advantage.

"Son, go to your corner and get that cleaned up," the referee demanded.

With a huff, Ron obeyed. As he walked back to his corner, he noticed Nick and his dad sitting tensely at the side of the mat. They looked concerned. He didn't know whether this was due to his bleeding or his pending run-in with Coach Granger.

"Forty-eight seconds," Granger growled from Ron's corner as the boy approached. "Forty-eight seconds for you to get your act together and turn him."

That was the style difference between Granger and Ron. His coach was always trying to make him wrestle slow and steady. For Ron, it was not the way to win matches.

"Turn him? I'm not going to turn him..."

"You're not going to take him down again," Granger interrupted as Assistant Coach Dean stuffed a wad of cotton up Ron's nose. "You're currently tied. You turn him, get your points and wait this thing out."

"He's tired," Ron began to argue.

"And your bleeding just gave him time to rest! You turn him! If he's so tired that he clams up and gets called for stalling, that's one more point and a state title for us."

With a nose full of cotton, Ron looked at Assistant Coach Dean who nodded in agreement. Knowing better than to try to plead his case, he hurried back to the center of the mat. Simms took his time returning to the center. It was evident to Ron that his opponent had gotten the chance to catch his wind.

With Tony once again set in bottom position, the referee invited Ron, "Top man on."

As Ron mounted, the noise around him suddenly disappeared. The only sound he heard was the referee's voice, "Ready... wrestle."

The flurry that followed lasted only seven seconds. Simms attempted to get up while Ron worked to break him down. The two boys ended at the edge of the mat and were called out of bounds. Ron looked at the scorers' table. The score of ten to ten gave him an incentive to rush back to the mat's center.

As Simms sluggishly followed, Ron looked to his corner and pleaded, giving Coach Granger the 'push away' sign. If he could only get permission to let his opponent go, he knew that he could take the boy down again and win the match, twelve to eleven.

Granger's only response was a glare as he pointed at Ron to mount.

"Top man on!"

As Ron mounted, he felt the anger swell inside of him. Who was Granger to decide how he would wrestle this match? Yes he was the coach but, realistically, this was the last match of the season. It wasn't like there would be an opportunity for the coach to suspend him from the team for insubordination.

Lost in his own little world, Ron's attention changed directions as he heard the words, "Ready...wrestle!"

Again Ron frantically tried to turn Simms to his back while the boy desperately tried to get away. As he tried a number of holds to try and gain control, Ron failed to get a firm grip on his sweaty opponent who was nearly hyperventilating. Fourteen seconds later, the two ended their rally off the mat again.

Quickly getting to his feet, Ron looked at the clock, which now read twenty-seven seconds. He looked to Granger and again, with a pleading look, gave the 'push away' sign to which Granger angrily mouthed "NO!"

"Top man on!"

Ron walked over to Simms and began to mount. "No!" he thought and got back to his feet.

With a quick glare at Granger, Ron positioned himself in a standing position behind Simms. He placed his hands flat in the middle of Simms' back, thumbs touching. He would let his opponent go, giving the boy a single point, and then take him down to get two points and the win. It was time for Ron Castle to wrestle his match.

"Ready...wrestle!"

Ron pushed Simms away and the boy sluggishly turned to face him.

"Escape! One point green," exclaimed the referee.

Ron failed to notice the roar from the crowd. His focus was on Simms' legs. As he shot for a 'single leg', Simms sprawled to his belly. Ron, caught underneath, rotated out and let go of the leg, getting to the open mat in the process.

As Simms sluggishly got to his feet Ron grabbed his wrist. Instinctively, Simms jerked his hand back, exposing his legs. This time, Simms reacted too late for Ron's single leg shot. Ron rotated behind Simms who quickly fell to the mat.

"Takedown! Two points red!"

In a last desperate act, Simms heaved himself sideways, his momentum carrying both himself and Ron out of bounds.

The referee's whistle split the silence and broke Ron back into reality.

Ron rushed back to the center of the mat with blood dripping from the bottom of the cotton wedge in his nose. He was barely able to contain the excitement within him. There were six seconds left on the clock. All Ron needed to do was break his weakened opponent down and hang on.

With the rest of the world so far away, it took him a moment to focus on the hand grabbing his elbow.

"Go get cleaned up," the ref's voice echoed as he steered Ron back to his corner.

In a fog of glory, Ron rushed back to his corner, not even noticing Nick and their father cheering from beside the mat.

Coach Dean toweled him off and replaced the cotton as Granger sat back in his chair and looked on intensely. Ron didn't really notice either of them. In six seconds, he was going to be the first sophomore state champ in Riverside High School's history.

With a fresh wad of cotton filling his nostril, Ron sprinted back to the center of the mat. This was it. This was his night. Tonight, he would show the state that he was the best.

"Top man on." The ref's voice sounded distant as Ron mounted. "Ready...wrestle!"

A flurry followed as Simms tried to stand with Ron fighting to hold on. He could feel the seconds ticking away as Simms dragged him toward the edge of the mat. Ron let a confident smile slip out as he focused on what getting to the edge of the mat would mean; starting again from the center with no time left. It was a sure state championship for Ron.

For a brief moment, Ron felt as if he were floating. Then, all too suddenly, the realization jolted through him. Simms was no longer under him. As the side of Ron's face crashed into the mat, he saw stars and lost his breath. Helplessly, he felt Simms complete the standing switch, ending up in control.

The referee's call of, "Reversal! Two points green," followed immediately by the sound of a foghorn, did not register for several seconds. Even when Simms dismounted and jumped around the mat in victory, all Ron could feel was a surreal sense that something had gone horribly wrong.

He looked up groggily. Things seemed to move in slow motion as Ron staggered back to the center of the mat to shake his opponent's hand.

As the referee raised Simms' hand in victory, Ron was already blearily walking back toward his warm-ups at the edge of the mat.

It had not been his night, the night he had dreamed of for so long. Tomorrow, he would begin to focus on next year's season and realizing that dream.

Chapter 2

He was running again, feeling the brisk wind braise his cheek as he picked up speed, racing along the banks of the coulee. Unlike most people, he was not captivated by the beauty of the scene; the light frost which covered the grass, catching rays of the rising sun. He didn't even notice. His thoughts were elsewhere, focused on a prize and the hunt that would officially begin tomorrow, the first day of practice.

An onlooker would have noticed that the boy's stride was not elegant. His steps were choppy and unbalanced, his breath visible as a light cloud of smoke in the crisp morning air. Yet, if it was grace he lacked, he more than made up for it with desire.

"Castle Wins State." That is what the headline would read. It would be an issue of the newspaper that he would be glad to deliver to anyone and everyone, not just those on his daily newspaper route. He had always hoped for a headline of "Castle Brothers Win State", but this was not to be. The boy cringed as he let his mind float. In all prior seasons, his brother Ron had been there, pushing him, goading him and making him better. Now those days were over.

Nick foggily remembered that night seven months earlier, his mother getting the phone call, the family racing to the hospital and sitting in the waiting room all night. He remembered Craig Helgeson's apology for driving recklessly and he remembered the parents of some of the other passengers from Craig's car berating Craig for his carelessness. Strangely, what he remembered the most was the smell when he walked into his brother's intensive-care room sometime mid-morning. It was a sickening hospital smell that made him vomit on the floor as his mother cried and his father tried to hold both his wife and Nick together.

Nick didn't need to see the wreckage of the Trans Am, the metal body of which had to be torn apart to get the victims from the back seat. When he saw his brother, he saw all he needed to see. Ron's face had only minor cuts and bruises but the tubes and wires connected to his body told the story. The boy clung to life with the ferocity with which he pursued everything else. For whatever reason, Nick didn't remember the doctor telling his family that Ron's spinal cord had been severed and that the boy would never walk again. Unfortunately, it was a truth that they all had lived with every day since.

Now, as his feet crunched through the light snow, Nick just wanted the season to start. He was tired of waiting for the state championship that he and Ron had talked about and dreamed about for as long as he could remember. He was ready for that journey, despite comments from some of the senior wrestlers that Nick would be lucky to make varsity.

This was Nick Castle's life. He was a competitor full of heart, but lacking the talent of his older brother. Now, just a day away from starting his sophomore season, he was focused on following in Ron's footsteps and bringing home the state title that had eluded his brother the prior season. In the minds of everyone but Nick, it was a prize significantly out of his grasp.

With visions of takedowns, reversals, wins and pins filling his mind, Nick turned the corner that led to the final quarter mile of his morning run. He broke into a sprint, picking up speed with each step. His lungs would be burning by the time he entered the driveway of the house on the outskirts of town but it didn't matter. All that mattered was the prize he sought.

Chapter 3

Nick peered into the classroom and walked on by. He knew he would eventually have to enter, he just wished that it could be under better circumstances.

"Every journey starts with one step," he told himself. Why was this step such a difficult one to take?

He was very good with people once he got to know them. Why did he have to be so shy about meeting people? In junior high, this hadn't been an issue as he had just followed Ron and instantly been accepted. Now with Ron taking all of his classes through private tutors to allow him more flexibility for rehab, Nick was on his own.

"Hey Castle, aren't you going to the meeting?"

The voice caught Nick by surprise. He turned around to see Oscar Black strolling up to him with his typical obnoxious smirk.

"Of course," Nick replied, turning a light shade of red.

While it was better than walking in alone, Oscar would not have been Nick's first choice of company with whom to enter the team meeting. The boy was disliked by most-everyone on the team, especially the seniors. He was cocky without reason and enjoyed using his runt size to his advantage, knowing that if he taunted larger students, they had a choice of looking bad by doing nothing or looking bad by beating up someone far smaller than themselves.

"I figure I've got the 112 spot locked up," Oscar commented.

"Uh, huh," was all Nick could muster as the two entered Coach Granger's Chemistry classroom. If Oscar couldn't make varsity at 112, he had better look for a different sport. Riverside High School had a void of wrestlers competing for the lower weight classes. There had even been talk about bringing up some junior high wrestlers to fill in gaps. Oscar could probably make it down to 103 with a little work. However, the smaller boy had never been known for his work ethic.

Oscar continued rambling with Nick only half-listening. The boy looked around the room at the familiar faces that he knew mainly through Ron's stories and experiences a few years back in junior high.

Weighing around 225 pounds, senior Dino Benz was the first person to stand out. He was an intimidating mountain of a kid Nick had never actually met but knew plenty about. Nick remembered being a seventh grader and watching Dino, then a freshman, dominate when his Roosevelt Junior High team came to wrestle against Nick's Lewis and Clark Junior High. Dino did not lose a match against junior high competition that year.

More impressive had been Dino's high school career. As a sophomore, he had been beaten out for varsity at 215 by an upper classman and was forced to wrestle heavyweight. Dino had placed fourth at state that year despite weighing an average of 40 pounds less than most of his opponents. As a junior, Dino had placed second in the state at 215 pounds and was considered the team's greatest hope for a state title this year. He sat quietly as Nick and Oscar entered, giving no acknowledgement of their existence.

"Junior varsity attendance isn't mandatory, but we're glad you could make it, Castle and Black."

Nick didn't need to look to see who had made the comment. Joel Vassec had been picking on him since elementary school. Why would he stop now?

Nick looked across the room to Joel's table and was able to force out a, "Hi, Joel," before looking away. Joel looked impeccable, as usual, with his jet-black hair and his fashionable clothes. He sat with Todd Mack, the senior Nick would have to challenge for the varsity spot at 135, and Joel's younger and much larger brother Clifford, a heavyweight. Nick and Oscar would certainly not be joining them at their table for this meeting.

Oscar, in his usual quick-minded way, rebuked Joel's comment by commenting loudly to Nick, "Wow Castle, I usually have to squeeze Vassec's head to get crap out of him." Nick cringed as he wondered what Joel would do to make Nick pay for his assumed partner-in-crime's reply.

Joel was a year older than Nick's brother, Ron, but the two had been best friends for ten years. In all that time, Nick had never liked him. Now, without the possible threat of falling out of favor with Ron, Nick was expecting the boy's tormenting to be full-bore. It was Ron who had talked Joel into coming out for wrestling in the first place. Now, as a senior at 152 pounds, the boy was sure to place at state.

Why couldn't there be an empty table? Nick just wanted a place to sit where he didn't have to confront anyone. As Nick pondered standing against the back wall, Oscar butted in on a half-full table. "Hey guys, Castle and I are going to join you."

Nick watched the boys' eyes roll as Oscar sat down.   He wondered if Oscar could have picked a worse table other than Joel's.   At this particular table sat Kevin Hermanns, the junior most likely to fill the 145-pound varsity spot and senior Colin Bradford who was considered to have a lock on varsity at 140 pounds.   In short, they were the two wrestlers most likely to be paired with Nick in practice.   He cringed at the thought of what these older boys might do to him if Oscar irritated them on Nick's behalf.

"Gentlemen!"

Even the sound of Coach Granger's gravely voice was welcome to Nick if it meant keeping Oscar quiet.

"I use the term loosely with most of you," the coach continued as he glared in Vassec's general direction.

"The first thing you need to realize is that nobody is guaranteed a varsity spot on this team.   Even fat guys that were runners up at state last year," he cast a cold stare toward Dino, "should realize that I will bring competition in from the halls, streets and alleys to challenge them."

Nick noticed that Dino just looked on, visibly not concerned by the coach's threats.

"We will practice every night that we don't have a match.   We have a new assistant coach this year named Sean MacCallister who could not be here for this meeting.   He will run morning conditioning practices for those of you who are having trouble making weight or need to improve your stamina.   Looking around, that appears to be the case with everyone in this room."

As he handed a stack of papers to the first table, he continued his speech.   "I'm giving you the schedule today because I want you to note that our first dual is two weeks from tomorrow against Sacred Heart.   That doesn't give you much time to get into respectable shape.   Any questions?"

Nick was glad to see that the meeting would be over quickly. He had been worried that the coach might make everyone introduce himself and he breathed a sigh of relief at not having to spend any time as the center of attention.

Looking around the room and seeing no questions, the coach continued.   "Seeing no questions..." the coach paused and Nick froze as he noticed the man was staring right at him.   "Are you little Castle?"

Nick's heart jumped into his throat as he felt all eyes in the room focus on him.

"Y…Yes," he stammered.

"How is your brother?"

Nick's mind went blank. What kind of question was that? His brother couldn't walk. That was bad. Should he say, 'bad'? However, Ron had been diligent about going to rehab. That was good. What kind of a reply made sense?

"I don't know."

As the only words he could think of left his mouth, he realized that they were about the worst ones he could have come up with.

Joel Vassec laughed out loud. "You don't know? Don't you live with him?"

Nick's face turned red as he scrambled for a follow-up comment.

"I mean he's doing alright. He's…in rehab. He says 'Hi'."

Nick looked down at the table, mortified at having been put on the spot like that. The coach cut in, "He was a tough kid. Give him my regards."

Then, seeing no need to take up any more of his time, Coach Granger adjourned the meeting.

Chapter 4

He was running again, making good time as he sprinted across the snow. It was soothing; the crisp air was refreshing on his lungs. As Ron looked down, he noted that he was only wearing his pajama bottoms. "How odd," he thought as he raced past the woods, suddenly aware that he was not alone.

The sweat was cold on his body as the boy picked up speed. His blood froze in his veins, as he wondered if he had the ability to out-run whoever or whatever was in those woods. He looked back quickly and immediately tripped over a small log. Scrambling to his feet, he continued his run, becoming ever increasingly more terrified and desperate.

The sight of the Castle house in the distance gave him hope but did little to calm his fears. Entering his yard, he was relieved to see the apparition losing ground. He was only a hundred yards from safety when he finally let a thankful smile cross his lips.

Ron would enter through the back door. Surely his parents would be livid if they knew he was out this late. Rounding the corner, he tripped on something metal. Upon closer examination, the object was his wheelchair and Ron's legs were caught in its straps. He was only able to drag it a couple of feet before the apparition was upon him.

"Dad!" he yelled.

The sound of Ron's own voice awakened him. He lurched up in bed, still trembling from the dream and now self-conscious as to whether or not anyone had heard his scream.

In the dim moonlight, his wheelchair lay beside Ron's bed. Ron angrily pushed it away and rolled over to face away from it. "Stupid piece of metal," he thought. The chair symbolized everything that was wrong with him. It kept him from practicing with his team today, winning his state title and living his life.

Still breathing heavily with his heart racing, he closed his eyes to try and go back to sleep.

Chapter 5

Somewhere in the darkness, Sean MacCallister heard a click. As the cobwebs cleared from his head, he knew his alarm clock now read 5:30. It was always the click that woke him up. He lay calmly, waiting for the music to initialize and the Gear Daddies' *Cut Me Off* to blast from the device.

As the guitar intro began, the young man soaked it in for a moment and smiled to himself before groggily getting out of bed. He felt good this morning, better than he had in years. He couldn't quite put his finger on the cause. It certainly wasn't his love life. His recent relationship, if one could call it a relationship, with Mandi Isaacson had ended poorly. In addition, his car looked to be barely road-worthy and his bank account was all but depleted.

Yet, despite all of this, the young man was content, the likely cause being his pending return to the wrestling mat, this time as an assistant coach. In preparation for this position, he had been working out for the past few months and the physical routine had really helped to clear his mind.

As he crossed the partial divider that separated the bunk beds from the 'entertainment area' of the room, he wasn't surprised to see Kelly passed out on the couch with the television still on. Kelly loved his TV. Sean was sure that the big man's eyes had been glued to some worthless program when he passed out. A variety of empty beer cans and bottles were strewn about the coffee table and the floor. The irony of the situation was not lost on Sean as he mumbled along with the song, "but you know when the lights go on and the beer is gone, it's still got a hold on me."

It was Kelly who had begun playing the song over and over again when Sean was going through detoxification several months earlier. This morning, it was clear that Kelly would be the one in need of losing some toxins.

As Sean reached over and took the half-empty bottle that Kelly still held in his hand, the big man looked up, still very drunk. "Late night, last night," Kelly commented.

"I noticed."

Even for Sean, who could sleep through almost anything, it would have been impossible to not notice the events of the prior night. His roommate had hosted ten to twenty people over the course of the evening, one of whom was passed out with his face buried in Sean and Kelly's second couch.

This was a typical night at the Beta Beta Beta fraternity. While the fraternity was a brotherhood of gentlemen and scholars, it was no stranger to alcohol and parties.

"Who is that?" Sean asked, motioning to the figure on the couch.

As Kelly squinted, looking toward the couch, it was clear that the identity of the person was a mystery to him as well. "I don't know," he answered as he stretched a bit.

"Good old Kelly," Sean thought. The man knew how to throw a party and was never afraid to lend a hand, a beer, or a couch to a stranger in need. While his hulking figure and obnoxious demeanor had put many people off, he was the only person in the world that Sean truly trusted. He was a faithful friend and, given Sean's estrangement from his father, the only male in the world whom Sean considered family.

Sean shook his head as he walked to the calendar for his morning ritual. Using a red pen, he wrote "126" on Monday, November 10th, adding another day to the sequence.

"How many are you up to?" Kelly inquired.

"One hundred and twenty-six days. I'm now five and a half hours into one hundred and twenty-seven."

Sean smiled as he thought about his impressive feat. It had now been over a third of a year since he had consumed an alcoholic beverage, no small accomplishment considering his living arrangement and previous three years as an alcoholic.

"You're wasting the best years of your life."

The banter, practiced almost daily, had started.

"But I feel better than you do this morning and will make it to class," Sean replied.

"See? 100% downside, no upside."

"I'm not in jail, either."

"Okay, I'll give you that one."

Sean paused briefly as he thought about his prior sentence. He didn't remember much about his last night of intoxication. He remembered a party in some small town and some thug making offensive remarks. What he didn't recall was the man hitting him or the ensuing fight that ended with the man's jaw broken and cheekbone shattered.

Even at a weight of 150 pounds, Sean MacCallister was not a man to provoke when he was drunk. He didn't talk openly about his high tolerance for pain or the pent up rage that enabled him to inflict pain on an aggressor. This combination had caused altercations of this sort to be far from infrequent during his drinking years. If not for the protection of his fraternity brothers, Kelly in particular, Sean would have likely suffered serious injury or worse prior to his twenty-first year.

"…Oooh… maybe that 'feeling better than me' part is an upside too," Kelly commented as he stumbled to his feet. He paused briefly to look at the body on the other couch. "I think he might be a roommate of one of the pledges. It looks like he wasn't in driving condition."

"Or walking condition for that matter," Sean added.

As Kelly crawled into his bed, a mattress on the floor under Sean's raised bunk, Sean was thankful that his friend didn't have to climb into a loft to get some sleep.

* * *

The ceramic tiles burned cold on Sean's feet as he walked into the bathroom and put his toiletries and alarm clock, still blasting out the Gear Daddies, on the sink. As he looked at himself in the mirror he was surprised to see the door open and Randy Hordelman walk in.

"Why are you up so early?" Sean's voice may have been a bit too chipper for his groggy friend.

The combination of lack of sleep and too many beverages forced Randy to lean against the wall to steady himself in front of the toilet. "It's 5:30. I've got to do my business. You're actually getting 'up' up?"

Sean turned on the shower and tested the water prior to hanging his BBB boxers on the hook outside. "I start my new job today," he replied as he stepped into the stall and shut the door. "I'm starting a new morning routine for finishing my homework."

The toilet flushed.

"Ow!" Sean yelled as the water suddenly turned scalding hot. He should have known better than to think he could shower in peace with the fraternity's prankster in the room.

"Hot one!" Randy called, intentionally giving the warning too late.

"Thanks for the warning," Sean's sarcastic reply came from somewhere inside the cloud of steam.

"Sorry."

As he pressed himself against the shower wall, waiting for the water temperature to normalize, Sean wondered if Randy truly might be sorry. Despite his selfish ways and constant tormenting of other members, Randy had proven to be sincere and forthright in all of his dealings with Sean to date.

As Randy washed his hands, Sean noticed the man checking himself out in the mirror. Randy had an almost model-like face to match his solid physique. His presence at a Beta Beta Beta party ensured at least a dozen extra women would be present. It was this kind of magnetism that made Sean want to keep Randy away from his little sister, Amy. Even though she was many miles away, Sean could not stop being overprotective of the young woman, a trait he had developed as a child.

"Do you start your coaching job today?" Randy asked.

"Yeah," Sean replied, smiling to himself.

"Do you know that pledge, Otis, very well?"

The sudden change of subject surprised Sean.

"We have to get rid of that guy." Randy commented and walked out the door.

Yes, Sean knew him. Otis Aamodt was a quiet kid from Louisiana, trying to survive a freshman course-load while battling his first winter in the frozen north. In Sean's opinion, the fraternity could do a lot of good for Otis. Sean would have to catch Randy later to make sure that he knew that the young man, although slow to speak, had a great deal of potential as a future leader.

"I'm glad somebody gave me a chance," Sean thought as he stepped back into the stream of water and continued his shower.

Chapter 6

Nick rounded the corner and broke into a sprint. He was a good ten strides behind Kevin Hermanns and could sense someone on his heels.

In all, the first day of practice had gone well for him. The team had started with warm-ups and 20 minutes of live wrestling and then moved straight into conditioning. Nick was very thankful for the daily runs he and his dog Chewie had made over the last three months when he noticed big Clifford Vassec barfing in a trashcan fifteen minutes into the first sprinting drill.

No, this would not be a pleasant day for those who had let themselves go during the off-season. Coach Granger had lived up to that promise.

The person behind him pushed Nick, causing him to have to adjust his balance. As he did so, Joel Vassec passed him and yelled, "Too clumsy for varsity!"

Nick fumed at the foul but wasn't surprised that it had come from Joel. Less than two hours into the season and he was already tired of the senior who had commented to the team in the locker room that the only reason Nick was being allowed to practice at all was as a gift for all of Ron Castle's past contributions to the team. Nick picked up his pace further as he needed to stay on Joel's heels. He planned to re-pass the older boy during the final lap and show that he could best him at something.

As they reached the final staircase, Nick saw an opportunity to gain ground. His long legs made him look like a gazelle, hurdling three stairs at a time and getting close enough to touch Joel's shirt. He considered pushing the boy as payback but thought better of it.

Such was Nick's life. As much as he wanted to, he never took a cheap shot. It wasn't only in wrestling. He thought of Todd Johnson, a big dufas his own age that, along with his cronies, enjoyed tormenting Nick in Biology class, Gym class and anywhere else that they crossed paths. Despite a 60-pound weight difference, Nick was sure that he could clobber the boy in a fistfight but there was always the worry of what the consequences would be: suspension from school, removal from the wrestling team, further tormenting by Todd and his friends?

Why did the unknown always have to keep him down? Ron always said that Nick spent so much time thinking about what the future might hold that he never let himself do anything in the present.

As Nick reached the top of the stairs, he had pulled even with Joel. Both boys broke into a sprint as they saw their coaches at the far end of the hall. "Hermanns first!" Granger's voice echoed down the corridor. "Pick it up, you two."

Joel leaned into Nick again as the two raced toward the finish line. Nick lost a step but stayed close to the senior's left side, nipping at his heels. In the final 20 yards, Nick gave his last extra surge of speed, pulling even with Joel as the two fought for position. As they crossed the finish line, he was deflated when he heard Granger growl, "Vassec second by a nose. Castle third. Walk it off and cool down."

Nick and Joel joined Hermanns in the wrestling room, all three of them walking slowly in circles with their hands locked behind their heads, expanding their lungs for that extra gasp of air. Joel approached Hermanns, giving the boy a 'high five' as they met. He then turned his back so that they were both walking away from Nick. "My money is on Mack for 135," Nick heard Vassec comment.

"Benz fourth!" Granger's voice echoed again from the hall. "Bradford fifth! Get moving you guys! You are obviously out of shape if fat Benz is ahead of you! You will not be running out of gas when we wrestle Sacred Heart in two weeks. Mack sixth!"

As these next three wrestlers entered the wrestling room and walked over to Vassec and Hermanns, suddenly Nick felt very alone. He was the only sophomore who had been able to keep up with the upper classmen, even beating some of the top-ranked wrestlers in the state. He wondered what it would take to finally earn their respect and get into their 'club'.

It was this thought that he pondered as he walked in a circle, letting his body recover from the afternoon's workout.

Chapter 7

Reluctantly, Nick entered the rehabilitation clinic. Why couldn't his brother just come out on his own? Why couldn't his dad go in and let Nick wait in the car?

He knew he shouldn't complain. It was just that he had a lot on his mind this night. Vassec's torments were keeping him isolated enough and now he was starting to get flack for being friends with Oscar. It made his head hurt. Nobody else seemed to want to hang out with Nick but they insisted on giving him a hard time about the one person that did seem interested.

It was an annoying problem and Nick didn't seem to have any answers. Maybe Ron would. His older brother had never had a problem fitting in. Maybe this was a good time to seek his advice.

Nick walked down the long hall until he found the right room. Peering in, Nick got chills as he saw the trainer stretching Ron's legs. Those legs that had once been so sculpted and powerful now seemed very sickly and skinny.

"Can you feel that?" the trainer asked.

Ron had an irritated look on his face, as he replied, "No."

"After your next surgery, some of that nerve blockage should be repaired and you should get some feeling back. Your leg muscles have deteriorated. But don't worry; we'll get them back. I've had patients recover to the extent that some even walk with braces and a walker."

Nick stood silently in the doorway, watching the two. He remembered his brother shooting in on opponents and lifting them in the air prior to driving them to the mat. With all of that talent bottled up inside a body that no longer functioned, Nick's issues suddenly seemed small.

The trainer handed Ron a weight for doing crunches. Neither of them even seemed to notice that Nick was in the room. At least, if Ron did notice, he wasn't acknowledging it.

"These will help build your abdominal muscles. I'll also show you other exercises for your lower back too. You're ready for these a lot sooner than I thought you'd be. Having strong muscles on both sides of your spine will add support."

The commentary seemed unnecessary. Ron was doing the crunches before the trainer even started the sentence. With the focus and effort his brother was putting forward, Nick wondered if it might be a while until Ron looked his direction. He was really hungry after the day's long practice. He cleared his throat to make his presence known.

Looking in Nick's direction, the trainer declared to Ron, "Time for you to go, champ. I'll show you those lower back exercises tomorrow."

Without changing his intensity level, Ron fired back, "Just three more sets."

"Dad's waiting in the car," the younger boy clarified.

Completely livid, Ron shouted, "Three more sets!" without even acknowledging his brother's presence with eye contact. The trainer, reluctantly, got down to help Ron as Nick dejectedly walked out of the room. Apparently his question about fitting in would have to wait until a later time.

Chapter 8

Sean sat back on his couch, feeling relaxed and relieved. It was nearing 11:00 p.m. on an evening that had started with a 7:30 phone call from Otis, one of the fraternity's pledges. Over the phone, Otis had intimated to Sean that he didn't feel that he fit in at the fraternity and was going to end his pledge-ship.

This decision had bothered Sean for several reasons. First, he knew of several members' unwillingness to get to know Otis and their mild dislike for the young man due to his unusual ways. Second, and more importantly, he had heard that Otis had faced greater obstacles while trying to fit in at the residence halls and feared that if he left the fraternity, he would likely leave college altogether.

The situation had struck a chord with Sean as he had been in similar straits a year earlier. Having already left one university to get away from memories of altercations caused by a year of heavy drinking, Sean had been on the verge of an untimely release from his pledge-ship as well the prior December after unwittingly kissing an active member's girlfriend during a chapter dance. Only the intervention of Kelly and several of Sean's other pledge brothers had saved his skin. Upon reflection, their actions had likely saved his life as the fraternity had provided the one stable environment that had allowed him to alter his self-destructive course.

Now, looking back on this evening's events, Sean didn't know how things could have turned out any better. He had invited Otis over and gotten the young man thoroughly engaged in a conversation about the fraternity being a place to gain leadership skills, not just a location to drink to excess.

Almost as if on cue, Randy had stopped in to borrow some ice from Sean's mini-fridge for his latest prank. While filling an over-sized beer mug with water and ice, Randy explained to Otis about the house's plumbing and how flushing any random toilet caused the showers to instantly turn scalding hot.

This lyceum continued as Randy led Otis to the bathroom, adding some obscure nonsense commentary about how the whole plumbing system had been developed by the ancient Incas, flushed the toilet and yelled, "Hot one."

The steam billowed from the shower as today's prank victim, Darrel, screamed and pushed himself firmly against the shower door, away from the scorching hot water. On this cue, Randy poured the glass of ice water over the door, onto Darrel and yelled "Cold one!"

Darrel screamed a second time as the ice water drenched him. As he reflexively jumped away from the cold, he ran right back into the blistering stream from the shower, resulting in a third scream.

Randy was immediately out the door, down the hall and down the stairs as Otis shifted himself out of the path of the naked man in hot pursuit. Sean watched the pledge smile for the first time he could remember as he absorbed the comical nature of the situation.

Now, several hours later, Sean sat alone on his couch. Randy was off planning who knows what kind of mischief and Otis, after reaffirming that he had no intention of leaving, was downstairs studying with some other fraternity members and learning about scholarship opportunities.

Tonight, things had just had a way of working out.

Chapter 9

The buzzing continued its annoying journey and found its destination in Nick's ear, despite efforts of the youth to thwart it by covering his head with a pillow. He just wanted the noise to stop. Why wouldn't it leave him alone? His entire body hurt and it needed sleep.

Eventually, he gained consciousness enough to realize that the 'snooze' button was within range and, with a single tap, banished the noise for another nine minutes. Unfortunately, Nick's alarm clock wasn't the only entity in the house with the ability to wake a sleeping high school student. Within seconds of hitting the button, his mother's voice rang from the hallway. "Get up, Nicky. You're going to be late."

Begrudgingly, the boy rolled out of bed, dressed slowly and trudged down the stairs to brave the cold and deliver his newspapers, wishing he could be as cheerful as Chewie was each morning. Nick had named the dog after his favorite *Star Wars* character and found him to be as faithful a companion as his namesake both on his paper route and his daily runs.

Nick was surprised to find his father sitting in the kitchen, reading a copy of the paper which he had already snatched from Nick's bundles. 5:00 was awfully early for anyone to be up, especially someone who did not have to be awake.

"Your brother said he's sorry for yelling at you yesterday. He wanted you to know to not take it personally. I wanted you to know because I have a feeling that he won't tell you himself."

Nick suspected that his brother never felt bad about these things, yet how else would his dad know if Ron hadn't said something? Dad had a history of keeping peace in the household. Apparently, this conversation was the vehicle for doing so under the current circumstances. With Ron and Mom asleep or in other parts of the house, it left an opening for Nick to ask a question, which had been nagging him.

"Dad, do you think he'll ever walk again?"

"I don't know, Nicky," the man replied. "That accident damaged his legs but it also damaged his spinal cord. It's not something that most people recover from. The one thing that I do know: if there is a way to recover, your brother will find it. I didn't raise you boys to be quitters. I've always been proud that you guys have never let me down."

Nick smiled shyly, accepting the compliment and hoping that he could continue to live up to that expectation. For now, he had to focus on the expectations of his newspaper customers. Afterward, he would go to practice to try to meet his coaches' expectations, which would not be easy. He had weighed in at 142 pounds the previous day and had been measured as having less than nine percent body fat. Their expectation of him to get down to 135 pounds was going to take some persistence.

As he walked out the door into the bitter morning air, Nick thought about his brother and the difficulties placed on Nick, living in Ron's shadow. Nobody had ever told Nick that he had to be perfect, so why was it that he felt that everyone would judge him to be a failure if he didn't place at least second in the state this year?

Chapter 10

I saw Mandi this morning."

Sean always hated when Randy brought up sore spots, most of which revolved around Sean's multiple failures in the area of romantic relationships.

"Let me guess, she's looking good."

Randy's grin was that of the Cheshire Cat, "Oh yeah. You should have kept her around a little longer."

"I didn't really have much say in the matter," Sean mumbled as the two walked on through the crowd of students who were using the student union as a 'warm up' stop on their way to class.

A face in the distance caught Sean's eye, giving him even more reason to be discouraged. If a discussion about Mandi was enough to bring Sean down, a run-in with Kevin Lakes would be enough to ruin his day completely.

The two were something less than acquaintances whose paths had crossed by some unfortunate fate ten months earlier when Sean, inebriated at a party, had fallen prey to the charms of a beautiful young woman named Candice who had taken him back to her apartment for a night of adult fun.

Exact details were fairly hazy, even the next morning. Sean remembered waking up wearing only his boxers in Candice's bedroom at about 3:00 a.m. when he heard pounding on her apartment door. Candice had gotten up to answer it and yelling ensued in the next room.

As Sean had hurried to pull on his pants and shoes, he pieced together through the wall the story that Kevin, apparently Candice's boyfriend, had just gotten back into town after a road trip with the university's hockey team. He accused Candice of cheating on him, a suspicion that she immediately revealed to be well founded as she confirmed it, mentioned that she hoped it had hurt him and punctuated it by informing Kevin that her latest love interest was still in the bedroom.

Sean stepped out and immediately apologized, which proved to be the wrong move as the bigger man lunged at him. Sean miraculously evaded Kevin's grasp and ran past Candice, out the door, with the hockey player in hot pursuit. Still half-naked, he weaved his way between houses and buildings and managed to lose Kevin on the two-mile journey before arriving home, half frozen in the frigid January air.

In the following weeks, he had come to realize how lucky he had been. Not only did Lakes have an ill temper in his personal life, the carry-over onto the hockey rink had earned him status as a leader in penalty minutes and a favorite among fans who judge hockey players by their willingness to take off the gloves and throw a punch.

Now, his mind returning to the present, Sean casually took off his watch, handed it to an unsuspecting Randy and dropped his book bag as Kevin Lakes attacked him in the middle of the crowd. Sean was ready for him, avoiding a punch by deflecting Kevin's arm upward and subsequently ducking behind the larger man, bear-hugging his waist and throwing him to the ground.

Caught in the rush of adrenaline flowing through his body, Sean punched Kevin in the side, knocking the wind out of him before he felt two powerful arms grasping him from behind and pulling him away. He struggled to get free but found himself completely immobilized in some kind of an arm lock.

Two men in their mid-forties grabbed Kevin and held him down as a string of obscenities poured from his mouth in Sean's direction.

"Just don't try to resist and I won't hurt you," a firm voice spoke into Sean's ear. "I saw the entire episode and I'll vouch for you as long as you're willing to let it go."

Sean let the tension drop from his arms as well as he could as he saw campus security arriving. They handcuffed both Sean and Kevin and led them off in separate directions.

* * *

Sean sat quietly, studying the man as he talked on the phone in the faculty break-out room. The cleanly-shaven bald head was the first thing most people would probably notice. In a baggy sweater and jeans, it was hard to judge his physical make-up but having been picked up off of the floor like a rag doll, Sean judged that the man was probably about as solid as granite.

"I understand. Good bye," the man said as he hung up the phone. He seemed irritated and impatient as he finally looked up at Sean.

"Campus police are on their way to take your statement," the man said, turning his attention to Sean. "A dozen witnesses have already corroborated your side of the story. You can press charges if you would like. I assume you know who he is."

"Yeah," Sean replied.

"You used some pretty impressive moves out there. It isn't just anyone who could get the better of a college hockey player of his size, especially one with his reputation for fighting. Did you wrestle in high school?"

"Yeah, and some in college."

"Not here apparently," the man continued. "My name is Cole Tyler; I'm an assistant coach for the university's wrestling team. Have you ever thought of trying out?"

The suggestion certainly hadn't been what Sean had expected and it gave him pause. If he could wrestle on scholarship, it would certainly lessen his monetary woes. Yet, at the same time, he would have to give up his current job and many of his campus activities. It just didn't feel like the right choice.

"I'm coaching over at Riverside right now and can't break that commitment, but thanks for the interest," Sean finally replied.

He felt slightly uneasy as Cole just nodded slowly with a look that Sean would describe more as 'focused' than 'disappointed'.

Chapter 11

Sean stretched out on the couch in the coaches' locker room, thumbing through a Calculus book that someone had left on the desk. The markings inside showed the deep frustration of some poor high school student who appeared to have been on the losing end of a fight with the material. As a college junior majoring in Engineering, the entire book seemed quite remedial to the young man.

It would be a long day. This morning's practice had been all aerobic as the wrestlers who were over their respective weight limits ran, jumped rope and did whatever else they could to ensure that, at weigh-in, the bar on the scale would drop. After an intensive two weeks practicing together, this would be the first time for this group to wrestle together as a team. The assistant coach was sure that stress was running high among certain wrestlers. He looked over the varsity roster:

Weight Class	Wrestler	Year
103	Derek O'Shea	Junior
112	Oscar Black	Sophomore
119	Jim Silver	Junior
125	Keith Wilson	Senior
130	Travis Skinner	Sophomore
135	Nick Castle	Sophomore
140	Colin Bradford	Senior
145	Kevin Hermanns	Junior
152	Joel Vassec	Senior
160	Arnie Bradford	Junior
171	John Jordan	Senior
189	Brian Keaton	Junior
215	Dino Benz	Senior
HWT	Clifford Vassec	Sophomore

The confrontation in the next room caught Sean's ear, causing him to look up from his light reading. Dino Benz uncharacteristically trudged into the office looking frustrated and annoyed.

"What's wrong?" Sean inquired.

"Freakin' Castle is fat by two and a half pounds. How could he be that heavy the day of the match?"

Sean wondered if anyone outside of the team could hear this conversation. 'Fat' was a term that was thrown around wrestling rooms that could be comical or confusing to untrained ears. Nick was little more than skin and bones at this point but still considered 'fat' since he was above his wrestling weight.

While Sean also was disappointed that Nick may not make weight, he didn't see a need for it to cause hostility. He had seen Nick work at practice. Nobody could claim that the boy's excess pounds were related to laziness or lack of effort. The kid was always one of the first to arrive and last to leave. Sean wondered if the boy just lacked the right experience.

"Maybe he just needs a role model to help him keep his weight down," the assistant coach countered politely. "I've seen more than one competitor in my day who struggled with getting his weight right at the start of the season and ended up eating double lunches on dual days before the conference tournaments came around. It seems to me that Castle could really use a friend at this point."

Sean suddenly felt guilty as he watched Dino's expression change from one of anger to one of shame. He didn't mean to bring the big guy down. He patted the boy on the shoulder as he crossed the room to get his coat.

Chapter 12

Nick adjusted his stocking cap and pulled the hood of his sweatshirt tightly over it. Clad in four layers of clothing, including a down jacket, sweat poured out of every pore in his body as the boy struggled to stay focused on jumping rope. Failure to do so would mean not making weight and the team having to forfeit the 135-pound weight class. It certainly wasn't how Nick wanted people to remember his first day on varsity.

"Twenty-three, twenty-four..." the boy counted. His mind wandered back to his morning weigh-in at which point he was two and a half pounds over. Of course, that had been after skipping supper the prior night, skipping breakfast that morning and running over a mile to school. Two and a half pounds over was certainly better than the five pounds he had been over the prior day, but over was over. He needed to find a way to make weight. He chose to work out over lunch instead of eating but it wasn't enough.

There were many things about Nick's sport that were undesirable, ranging from injuries to cauliflower ear and mat-borne infections. However, all of these paled compared to the misery of cutting weight. He hated the fatigue, not to mention the chapped lips and bad breath that were part of his life the day of the match, certainly making him even less attractive to the girls.

Nick picked up his pace. He had found a spot to jump in the boiler room. With time getting short, he knew he had to take drastic measures. After class ended at 3:30, he had still been nearly a pound over. Vassec had taken the opportunity to chew him out echoing Dino's sentiments from that morning.

"If you don't make weight, you don't wrestle," Vassec had growled. "It's not rocket science. You would think that Ron Castle's brother would know better."

It wasn't what Nick had needed to hear in his current state. Why did it always have to come back to him being Ron's little brother?

The other team would arrive for weigh-in around 5:00, giving him only an hour and a half to burn off, or more specifically 'sweat out', the rest of that weight. He knew he had to find strength to continue somehow but he stopped jumping and leaned against the wall, completely exhausted. He cradled his head in his arms as he leaned against the cement bricks. He didn't have strength to move, much less jump any more. He felt as if he could break down and cry at any time but he would not let himself do so. As he heard the door open behind him, he struggled to regain his composure before turning around to see who had joined him.

Nick's blood ran cold as he turned to see Dino coming toward him. "No," he thought. "Not another lecture. Please kill me instead."

"How much do you still have to lose?" the bigger boy asked.

"Three quarters of a pound," Nick replied, avoiding eye contact at all costs.

"Here," Dino said, handing Nick a water bottle. "Rinse out your mouth but don't swallow. I'll be back in a minute with a garbage can for you to spit into."

Nick didn't know what to think. Was this some kind of a trap? Were a bunch of the guys going to come in and taunt him for drinking water when he was still over weight? He waited until Dino re-emerged with a trashcan and a boom box before he allowed himself to take a sip.

It was paradise. As the cool liquid filled his mouth, every fiber in Nick's dehydrated body begged him to swallow. Somehow he resisted the temptation, swishing the heavenly liquid around and briefly gargling before spitting into the trashcan as it was presented. He didn't know what was up Dino's sleeve but he didn't care. For a few seconds on this dismal day, his mouth once again felt human.

Dino set the boom box down and plugged it in. "Do you like Judas Priest?" he asked.

Nick didn't really know much about the group but, at this point, he wasn't going to complain. "Sure," he replied.

As the music began to blare, Dino donned a jump rope and began jumping. Nick quickly fell in line beside him.

"I thought you were on weight," Nick inquired.

"I am," Dino commented, "but I'm still a little too close for comfort. Besides, I know that cutting weight alone can be miserable."

Nick couldn't disagree.

Over the next hour he jumped rope, jogged in circles and did sit-ups as he listened to the senior talk about A'Romano's Pizza Parlor, their special 'hot and spicy' pizza sauce and the joint's hot cashier, Cheri Winters. Nick had to smile at the stars in Dino's eyes every time he mentioned Cheri. She was a cheerleader who was part of the 'in crowd'. Nick knew that she was the kind who only dated the captain of the football team or the student body president, not necessarily an average guy like Dino. Still, it was clear that Dino thought the world of her.

The underclassman didn't get to talk much, nor did he want to. Somehow, he found the energy to shed the last bit of weight and, for the first time this season, he felt that he was not the only one on the team who wanted to see the name "Nick Castle" on the team roster.

Chapter 13

Nick cringed as he saw the mat rushing to meet him. There was a dull thud followed by the pain, as he was slammed down hard.

For a moment, he wished that he hadn't made weight. Upon seeing his opponent Trent Gallo at weigh-in, Nick had been worried. He was about three inches shorter than Nick with muscle mass to make up the difference and bring him to the same weight. He had Brillo-Pad hair and wild eyes that made Oscar comment, "That guy is an animal."

Oscar didn't know the half of it. Gallo didn't look nearly as strong as he actually was. Nick could hardly breathe as the boy wrapped him up and turned him to his back an instant before the foghorn sounded, ending the first period. It was the most beautiful sound Nick had heard in months.

Nick lay on the mat for a moment before staggering to his feet. Noting that he was only down by a score of one to seven made him feel a little better but it didn't take the full sting out of the fact that the match was only a third over.

He watched as the referee asked Gallo to choose his position for the second period and the boy deferred to Nick. Hoping to gain a point for escaping, Nick opted to start in the 'down' position and moved into place right away.

Nick cringed a bit as he felt Gallo mount, grabbing Nick right above the elbow. The ref blew the whistle and Nick clumsily tried to get to his feet before being dragged back to the mat and turned to his back once again.

From his spot on the bottom, Nick looked around in a daze. He saw the time clock and realized that he was either going to have to wiggle his way free or spend nearly two minutes on his back, fighting being pinned. He bridged the best he could as Gallo adjusted his weight so that it was all on top of Nick's chest.

Nick wanted to fight but was too worn down. The weight-cutting process had left his muscles fatigued, his body dehydrated and his spirit dampened. Unable to hold his own weight, much less the weight of the other boy, he finally collapsed.

The referee slapped the mat.

Nick had failed. His first match as a varsity wrestler had not only resulted in a loss, but a pin. This gave the opposing team six team-points, the same number that they would have gotten had Nick not made weight, causing his team to forfeit the weight class. Nick got to his feet, wondering why he even tried, as he shook his opponent's hand and watched the ref raise Gallo's arm in victory.

Granger didn't even look at Nick as he left the mat. Only Sean was there to pat him on the back quickly as the boy walked to the warm-up mat where Vassec, the last person Nick wanted to see, was stretching.

"We could have used a little bit more from you, Castle. Now we're down six to twenty-one. We don't have a lot of people left to pick up that slack."

Nick avoided eye contact as he put on his warm-ups. He knew he had wrestled poorly. He knew he had lost. And most of all, he knew he had let the team down. He did not need to be reminded of these facts.

As he walked back to his chair, dejected, he heard Vassec comment to Hermanns, "Why can't he be more like his brother?"

Nick was not naïve enough to believe that the remark was not meant for his own ears.

Chapter 14

Nick's body felt sore all over as he continued jumping rope with the team. Having lost the prior night's dual decisively, Granger had decided to make this morning's practice mandatory instead of optional, stating that anyone choosing to skip practice or take it lightly would be cut.

As most of the team worked on endurance, a single member at a time was called into the adjacent classroom to meet one on one with Granger to review the video of his match. Judging by murmurs from Oscar and others, these sessions were not going well. Nick quietly dreaded the fact that he was next in line.

"Keep moving, gentlemen," Sean commanded as he led the drills. "It's time to build your wind."

The assistant coach had been making his rounds, talking to each of the boys individually while giving direction to the group as a whole. Nick was glad to see that Sean did not appear to be angry as he addressed the 135-pounder.

"How did your first varsity match feel?"

"I lost." It was the only reply that Nick could come up with. He felt that he should at least acknowledge the truth.

"I know, but if you keep working hard, the wins will come. I noticed that you were the first one here again this morning, running laps before practice. That's a good start."

Nick felt good that at least one person could still find a bright side and reason for hope. He really was trying; it was just that Trent Gallo had squashed him flat, putting a damper on his ability to get the results he sought.

"Castle!" Granger's voice filled the air and Nick ran quickly toward the classroom door, trying to keep from angering the man any further.

Inside the classroom, the session started out with the coach commenting sternly, "We need more from you, kid. We can't have you flopping around on your back and giving up six points."

As the video rolled, the commentary got worse. Nick sat quietly and absorbed the verbal beating.

Chapter 15

Sean took a brief instant to look across the gymnasium. Six mats were laid out, each with a dual taking place on it. For a moment, he wished he could be at any mat other than the one in front of him. Unfortunately for Sean, he was dedicated to staying beside this match, even though it meant watching the painful sight of one of his most dedicated wrestlers, Nick Castle, taking the beating of a lifetime as he was dragged from one side of the mat to the other, being let up and then thrown back down again time after time after time.

It only took a few seconds from the time the initial whistle sounded for Sean to realize why Coach Granger had almost elected to forfeit the match rather than let Nick wrestle. His opponent, Tony Heidt, was ranked second in the state and was as aggressive a competitor as Sean had seen.

Sean could only stand and watch as Tony took a deep shot on Nick, taking the boy directly to his back. Unable to turn to his stomach, Nick could only strain to keep his shoulders from touching as the ref counted for the near-fall. Finally, after ten seconds, Tony let Nick roll through to his stomach.

"Two points green, takedown. Three points green, near-fall."

Sean looked up at the scoreboard. Tony was winning eleven to two with over half a minute still remaining in the first period. For the third time, he let Nick up and tousled the boy's hair for fun as he let him go.

"One point red," the ref declared.

It was clear to Sean that Heidt was not just here to win this match. He seemed to enjoy tormenting Nick, getting a thrill from embarrassing a weaker opponent. The boy laughed as he shot again, taking Nick hard to the mat and gaining control.

"Two points green, takedown."

Sean looked to his right where Granger was clearly angry. What was unclear as he stood at the side of the mat was whether the anger was directed at Nick for wrestling poorly or himself for letting this match take place.

Heidt put Nick in a half nelson, applying pressure to the back of the boy's neck to get him to turn.

"Nick, look away and peel! LOOK...AWAY...AND PEEL!!!" Sean yelled, trying to provide guidance on some kind of defense for his wrestler but it was too late. Nick's body was unable to counter the leverage of his opponent and he flipped to his back.

Nick fought valiantly for another few seconds but his opponent's grip was too tight and determination too much as he intentionally pressed his chest against Nick's mouth and nose, smothering the boy. Losing his last bit of strength, Nick's shoulders fell to the mat and the ref slapped the mat beside them, signaling the pin.

There was a fair amount of cheering from the opposing team's fans but what disturbed Sean was the fat kid in the Riverside section, along with a couple of cronies, who was actually booing Nick. He wished for a moment that he could teach these boys some manners.

Nick had won one match and lost three during this tournament. Unless things turned around in the higher weight classes, this dual would be the team's last of the day.

Sean patted Nick on the back as he walked off the mat. He did not use any words, because there were none that would change what the boy had just been through.

Out of the corner of his eye, he could see Joel Vassec giving Nick an earful of 'If you're not going to wrestle, why do you even show up?' and was glad to see Dino Benz pull the older boy away but, unfortunately, not before Joel commented loudly, "He's lucky that they even gave him the one win. He was stalling the whole third period."

Sean couldn't quite understand it. Nick matched up well against some of the top wrestlers near his weight in practice and clearly had the dedication, talent and heart to be a winner. There had to be a way for him to turn the corner.

As Nick sat down by himself on the stretching mat, put his warm-up jacket on and pulled the hood up to cover his head, Sean turned his attention to the 140-pound match.

Chapter 16

Sean's mind wandered. He appeared to be watching the championship dual as he sat, staring blankly into space. Upon hearing the clamor of big feet, he broke from his trance, looking up to see Dino Benz, of all people, joining him in the bleachers.

"You had a good tournament, shooter. Four and zero."

Dino only nodded in recognition of the compliment.

It really had been a long day. Sean was glad to have company that didn't appear to be eager to gab, giving him room to reflect on the day's events. Unfortunately for Sean and his tired mind, the initial silence was short lived and broken in a most unpleasant way.

"Coach?" Dino asked. "Why didn't you wrestle in college?"

It was a question that caught Sean off guard and one for which he did not have an answer suitable for high school ears to which he was supposed to be a role model. He certainly couldn't tell this boy that he had let drinking come first. He decided to evade the question by focusing on half of the story.

"I did wrestle my freshman year at Wisconsin. I red shirted for the first half of the season and was varsity after our 141-pounder got hurt… won eight, lost five. Then, my sophomore year rolled around and I ended up transferring schools and moving here. I decided to concentrate on school and other things."

He hoped that Dino would not sense anything missing or ask for clarification as to the 'other things'. To be safe, Sean quickly changed the subject.

"Are you going to wrestle in college?"

The look on Dino's face told Sean immediately that he had hit a sore spot.

"If I can go to college," was Dino's initial reply. It took him several seconds before he chose to elaborate about how his dad's store wasn't doing well but, because it was such a large asset, Dino had been rejected for financial aid. Certainly they couldn't be expected to sell the family business to put Dino through college, could they?

"Do you get any help from your parents?" Dino inquired.

This question too caught Sean off guard, biting hard into the young man's psyche. His relationship with his parents, or more realistically, the lack thereof was the thing that Sean discussed with nobody. Kelly knew bits and pieces due to some of Sean's drunken tirades a year earlier but even he did not know the entire story.

Nobody in Sean's family had seen or heard from his mother since she had abandoned them, nearly a decade earlier. His drunken, abusive father had raised Sean and his younger sister between several temporary moves to foster care and grandparents when things had gotten too rough. Sean liked to think that most of his physical scars had healed from those days but he knew that the emotional ones were there to stay. He was glad that, since his own escape from the liquor bottle, the memories had not resurfaced in the violent way they had in years past. His old man was a thousand miles away, out of sight and out of communication now for over a year and a half. This physical and communicative distance had been Sean's choice and he had never regretted it.

"No," Sean finally answered and again rushed to change the subject. "You know, you could get a scholarship."

"Yeah, but it doesn't seem like any recruiters are ever at our matches. At least, none of them ever talk to me," Dino commented, pointing down to where Cole Tyler and another university coach were sitting. "I've seen them at a couple of tournaments but they don't seem to watch our team at all. They used to come to watch Ron Castle last year."

Sean was a bit taken aback that college recruiters would come to watch a sophomore.

"He was that good, huh?"

"Yeah, he always knew what he had to do to win. Even the matches he lost, you always got the sense that he was going to find some way to come out on top. He was cocky but I think it served him well because he never believed that he could lose."

"A tough act for his younger brother to follow."

"Oh, yeah," Dino replied. "Nick walked into a weight class this year filled with guys that his brother humiliated last year. You can really see it in the way that guys like Tony Heidt go after him. I would hate to be in his shoes."

This explained a lot to Sean about Nick's final match of the day. It wasn't just that Nick had been completely worn-out from cutting weight: starving, running, jumping rope and whatever else. He had a number of people gunning for him to get their revenge. The weight challenges would be eased after Christmas when each weight class would increase by two additional pounds. However, this other issue likely would not.

Sean stared down at the university coaches and then looked Dino in the eye.

"We'll just have to find a way to make them watch you," he commented and patted the large boy on the back.

Chapter 17

The Biology teacher's voice droned on and on as Nick fought to stay awake. The 10:00 hour was always difficult for Nick. He liked his teacher, Mr. Garrett, well enough but the subject matter did not come naturally to him. Couple this with the facts that any adrenaline that may have been in his body from his morning practice had long since exited and that Todd Johnson sat in front of Nick in this particular class and it just did not add up to a pleasant time.

Nick's head bobbed for the third time and didn't come back up.

"Mr. Castle, perhaps you would like to tell us about the different types of cells."

The sound of his name lurched Nick back to consciousness. How long had he been asleep? What was the question? It was something about cells.

"I'm sorry, Mr. Castle. Am I keeping you awake?" the teacher continued.

Nick could feel himself turning red. He had been caught completely off guard. Now, everyone was looking at him as he struggled to comprehend what the question may have been.

"Pay attention, Castle!" Todd Johnson contributed loudly as his cronies snickered. "The rest of us are trying to learn something. You're holding us up."

Nick needed to focus and the extra commentary sure didn't help.

"You want to know about the kinds of cells?" Nick clarified.

"Yes."

Thinking quickly, he looked the teacher in the eye and answered, "Prokaryote cells are disorganized and have no nucleus. Eukaryote cells have a nucleus."

Any answer had to be better than no answer. If he was going to go down, at least he would put up a fight.

"Is he correct, Mr. Johnson?" the teacher inquired.

"No," Todd answered, more out of a sense of wanting to argue than having any clue as to the right answer.

"Really? I felt his answer was vague, but acceptable."

Nick let out a sigh of relief. He may not have won this match but at least he scored points.

As Mr. Garrett reached down to pick the doodle sheet off of Todd's desk, he formalized his requests. "Mr. Castle, please keep your eyes open while in my class. Mr. Johnson, please try to pay some sort of attention. You may learn something."

Chapter 18

Sean entered the wrestling room and paused for a moment to look around. The university had done well in its set-up. When Sean wrestled at his former college, his team was given temporary use of a few hundred square feet of space under the condition that the mats would be rolled up and stored away before the women's volleyball team moved in for their allotted time.

The room before him was state-of-the-art in Sean's mind. It was a dedicated wrestling facility with permanent mats, padded walls, several practice dummies and enough space for a few dozen wrestlers to train without fear of being accidentally squashed by adjacent teammates.

"A person could certainly do worse than this," Sean commented to himself.

Only one other person was in the room at this particular time but, fortunately, it was the person that Sean had hoped to find. The young man watched with intrigue as Cole Tyler dragged a practice dummy around the mat as if trying to gain leverage over an opponent. With cat-like quickness, the large man popped his hips and launched the dummy in a perfect head and arm throw. The dummy landed on the mat with a loud thud with Cole ending up on its chest.

"Two points takedown and three back points," Sean called out.

"He's stuck," Cole replied, not even looking Sean's direction.

The large man continued about his business, picking up the practice dummy and putting it against the wall.

"Is the coach around?" Sean inquired.

"He left about half an hour ago," Cole replied, still not making eye contact.

"I don't know if you remember me, my name is Sean MacCallister. I'm an assistant coach at Riverside."

The big man moved to a peg board on the wrestling room wall. He made it look easy as he pulled himself up, one peg at a time, reached the top and came down the same way, in a measured slow methodical manner. Reaching the bottom, he finally granted Sean a response.

"You got in a fight at the Union."

So he did remember. Of course, given the eerie fact that the man wouldn't look at Sean, he should have re-introduced himself as someone grander. The King of Spain, perhaps?

"Yeah, that's right." Sean stood uncomfortably, waiting for the bigger man to open up and say something else. He waited until the man finished his next exercise, 50 sit-ups. The man still didn't bother offering any kind of small talk. Sean decided to get to the point.

"Do you think you guys will have any interest in Dino Benz for next year?"

"He's ranked in state. If he continues to do well, we may look at him to walk on to the practice squad."

This, of course, wasn't the response Sean had hoped for. Dino needed a scholarship, not a spot as someone else's throw-dummy.

"One of the other top 215-pounders will be in town for a dual next Monday. It would be a good match for you to evaluate."

"I know how to do my job," the larger man rebutted. It was clear that he was irritated. He pulled out a ratty green duffel bag and began packing it.

"Anything else?"

Sean couldn't leave with nothing. He decided to go with his plan B for getting Dino noticed. "Do you know what the Christmas break practice schedule looks like?"

"Strength and conditioning every morning, technique every afternoon," the man replied coldly.

"Do you mind if I bring some seniors, Benz in particular, up for some extra practice? They could use some high-caliber competition."

"We'll see," was Cole's only response.

He picked up his gear and crossed to the entrance with Sean in tow, finally looking at the young man, catching him straight in the eye with an intense stare Sean felt uncomfortable returning.

"Your team isn't especially strong. I saw parts of several duals at the tournament last weekend. That was about all I really need to see. When you produce another Ron Castle and field a team with lots of shining stars, we'll show up. There is only so much time and money for recruiting."

As the two reached the door, Cole turned out the lights.

Sean reiterated the only thing he wanted Cole to remember, "I'll still hope to see you on Monday."

"I know," was the bigger man's only response as he turned and walked down the hall, away from Sean.

Chapter 19

Sean leaned back in the driver's seat and smiled. His Galaxie 500 was several decades old but she still had plenty of life left in her. Given Sean's financial situation, the old girl was obligated to keep kicking for at least another year and a half until Sean could graduate and afford to buy something newer.

He revved the engine, just to hear the eight cylinders roar to life. Yes, for all of her rust, scrapes and dents, she still had power and had never let him down. The question was, was she truly in better shape than Coach Granger?

The older man had been fuming as he walked over to Sean's vehicle twenty minutes earlier. Nick Castle's Algebra teacher had refused to let him re-schedule his test due to a recent incident involving stolen test answers and the basketball team. Lacking any other option, Granger had agreed to let Sean drive the boy the 75 miles to the dual. Seeing Sean's mode of transportation up close, he questioned his decision.

"Is it road-worthy?" the head coach had asked.

"She's in better shape than you are, old man," Sean had answered.

The young man's sarcasm had failed to improve Granger's disposition.

"If I wanted any crap out of you, I'd squeeze your head," the old man had snapped back. "I'm trusting a student to your care. If anything happens to him, I'll have your butt."

As Sean had opened his mouth to place a burn on the coach's last comment, Granger quickly cut him off. "Don't even..." he started, his face getting redder as he turned and walked toward the bus.

The vehicle was ready, as was the coach; all that was needed now was the passenger. Secretly, Sean was glad to have this opportunity to get to know Nick. The boy showed so much heart and determination at practice; Sean was always surprised how he fell flat when it was time for live competition.

Sean nearly burst out laughing as he saw Nick leave the school. He didn't know which was more comical, the half-dozen layers of clothing that the boy was wearing or the look on his face when he saw the condition of Sean's car.

"Let me guess, you're heavy," Sean commented.

Although Nick's sheepish look was confirmation enough, he insisted on a verbal reply as well. "I was a pound and a quarter over at lunch but I've got a stocking cap, two tee shirts, two sweat shirts, pants, sweat pants and this jacket."

It would be good for the boy to sweat during the trip. Sean handed him an extra large jacket he had found in the trunk. "It's my roommate's," the young man commented. "He won't mind if you sweat in it and stink it up. To tell you the truth, he probably won't even notice."

Nick looked very hesitant to get into the car. Fortunately Sean knew just enough about the boy to get past that stumbling block.

"She'll make point five past light speed," the coach commented. "She may not look like much…"

"…but she's got it where it counts," the two ended in unison. As Sean expected, the reference was enough to get the boy past the car's appearance and get him inside.

"You're a *Star Wars* fan?" Nick inquired, buckling his seatbelt.

"Who isn't," Sean replied, getting behind the wheel, ditching his jacket and cranking the heat.

"My job," he continued, "is to keep it hot enough in here so that you make weight. Your job is to sweat like crazy and be less than 135 pounds when you step on the scale in an hour and a half. Agreed?"

"Agreed," Nick confirmed.

Sean watched the awkward youngster out of the corner of his eye. Nick was clearly an introvert who wanted to be more social. Sean had sensed tension between Nick and some of his teammates from the beginning but, for the life of him, couldn't put his finger on what the boy had done to deserve any animosity.

Remembering his promise to his boss, Sean commented to Nick that the boy needed to inform his coach when issues like this test situation came up.

"Is he mad?" the boy asked.

Sean considered Nick's perspective for a moment. The wrestler likely felt he was being blamed for something beyond his control. Sean certainly didn't want to make him feel any worse than he already did.

"I don't know if I'd say he's mad. He's just frustrated that things like this come up unexpectedly and stressed that he then has to find solutions on short notice."

As Nick sat silently staring out the windshield, Sean hoped that he had softened the message enough. If the kid was too wrapped up in his own world, hearing things from the coach's perspective may not have resonated well. Sean was happy when the boy finally opened up again.

"He seems to be frustrated and stressed a lot. He never talks to me when I lose. It's like I'm not allowed to lose."

It wasn't the reply that Sean had expected. He had thought that Nick would be angrier at his teammates who ridiculed him after losing. Perhaps Sean needed to assume the role of 'supportive coach' if Granger wasn't filling it.

"Do you think it's because of your brother?" the coach asked.

"YES!!! Of course it is! He was perfect and I'm supposed to be perfect too," came the reply.

Sean was surprised again at how frustrated the wrestler sounded. He believed he was beginning to see a pattern. After watching his brother lauded as a hero for a year, poor Nick was starting at a deficit. Even winning half of his matches wouldn't be enough to gain Nick the notability and support that his brother had enjoyed. Could it be that the boy had been left with the impossible task of filling his own shoes as well as his brother's? He knew he had to come up with an answer quickly to keep from letting the boy down as nearly everybody else had.

"I never saw your brother wrestle," Sean admitted, "but I understand that he was something special. The thing is, you've got a lot of good tools and a ton of heart. I think that you're on the verge of carrying on the family tradition. I'm not saying that you're going to be a state champion this year, but I do know that you're a lot better than your record shows and a hundred times better than you're willing to admit to yourself."

Sean was so wrapped up in his speech that he didn't notice a large pothole in the road. His car's suspension groaned as he hit it, causing the whole vehicle to shudder. As Nick grabbed the armrest, it fell off in his hand.

"You're sure this thing is safe?" Nick asked, involuntarily changing the subject.

"Old Fords don't die, they just get faster," Sean replied with a grin.

"We aren't going to die, are we?"

Sean was quiet for a moment. There was a time in his life in which he had spent days pondering his own mortality. That was a dark period. He avoided the temptation of letting his mind wander there today. He couldn't let this kid watch him wallow in the darkness that fell over him when he dwelled on this subject.

"Kid, I'm going to die quietly, surrounded by family," the coach finally replied in a teasing voice, "not in a car wreck with a scrawny weasel like you. Then, they'll throw me in a hole in the ground, play Derek and the Dominos and go have a party."

Despite Sean's lack of family-style relationships, he really believed this to be true. He used the remainder of the trip to build Nick's trust that someone on the coaching staff was in his corner, literally and figuratively, and that wins were on their way soon if Nick continued to give his all.

Chapter 20

Nick fought being pinned with everything he had as his opponent used every means possible to hold the boy on his back. The irritating blare of the foghorn was the most welcome noise Nick had heard all evening.

"Three points green," the referee bellowed as the wrestlers climbed to their feet.

Nick watched the scoreboard change to a score of fifteen to eight as he shook the other boy's hand and watched the ref raise his opponent's arm in victory to the delight of the crowd. Nick was surprised that he didn't feel quite as bad as usual.

Was it because he hadn't been pinned? Losing by seven points certainly was nothing to be proud of, but at least he had only given the opposing team three points, the minimum number of team points possible in such a situation.

For a change, Nick had actually heard his coaches' voices as he wrestled. Coach MacCallister's voice in particular had resonated with him, guiding him on the right combination of moves needed to earn a takedown in the second period, giving Nick a temporary lead.

Nick watched the team score change to six points for Riverside and nineteen for the home team. He pondered the fact that two pins would be all it would take to get Riverside back within a point of the other team. Surely Dino could deliver one of those pins.

As Nick walked off the mat, still looking dejected, Granger ignored him as usual. However, the boy was relieved to see Coach MacCallister walking his way.

"You wrestled better," the assistant coach commented, patting Nick on the back. "You just need to move it to the next level."

Nick nodded in reply as he walked back to the warm-up mat to stretch. He couldn't put his finger on it but, for some reason, things seemed like they were starting to go his way.

Chapter 21

This ought to do it," Nick thought as he took Tom Mack down again. In the back of Nick's mind, the match score changed to eight points for Nick versus three for Tom. He heard Coach MacCallister's voice echo that score as he began working to turn Tom to his back.

Nick was wrestling with anger on this particular day. As usual, he was angry at Joel Vassec who had been taunting him for the past several days about how Tom was going to take Nick's varsity position. The current score of this wrestle-off made Nick beg to differ. He wished there was some way that he could rub Joel's face in this after the match was done but he knew that Joel would have some kind of comeback about Nick's poor varsity record. It just wasn't worth the time.

As if having to put up with Joel wasn't enough, Nick had suffered another run-in with bully Todd Johnson and his cronies this afternoon. The larger boy had pushed Nick from behind, sending him crashing into a row of lockers. As his body slammed into the metal, Nick was sure the entire school could hear the noise.

Beyond the physical tormenting, there had been several phrases thrown at Nick about how he sucked at wrestling and how their grandmas could have beaten the guy that beat Nick the other night. That cretin Tim Parks, Todd's greasy-haired miniature crony, had even hurled insults about Ron being crippled.

Nick was so furious and ashamed of himself that he could hardly stand it. All of it poured into this wrestle-off against Tom. The two usually wrestled close matches at practice but, on this day, Nick held a five-point lead and was intent on turning his opponent to put an exclamation point behind this win. The sophomore's adrenaline was still flowing when he heard Coach MacCallister blow the whistle, indicating that the contest was over.

Unfortunately, as Nick had his hand raised in victory, he knew that this feeling of satisfaction would be short lived. He knew that the team would leave the mat soon and the varsity wrestlers would have to weigh themselves in front of the coaching staff. With only three days to go until he had to weigh in for the dual, Nick had gone into the day's practice nearly ten pounds over weight.

"This is completely unacceptable!" Nick could already hear Coach Granger's words. "You had better be in here both days this weekend and not just for the pre-Christmas dance!" the man would continue.

Nick dreaded the subsequent few days. The weight-cutting regimen already made him feel weak. Yet he had held onto his varsity spot. Dropping those pounds was simply part of the game.

"You wrestled well, Nick. Let's bring that intensity to the dual on Monday," Coach MacCallister commented, patting Nick on the back.

Nick smiled shyly. He felt good about having this coach on his side. He just wondered how long that would last if he continued to struggle with his weight and lose matches.

Chapter 22

Nick stared across the room, not fully aware of his leg bouncing in a nervous twitch under the table. Oscar's voice echoed in his ears but Nick didn't hear the words. He sat quietly, thinking about Heather.

Nick had promised himself that he would ask her to dance today. It would have to be a slow dance as he really felt foolish during faster songs. Why was it that he could improvise on the wrestling mat without issue but, on the dance floor, every movement made him cringe with shame?

As the song ended, Nick tensed up. As his heart temporarily stopped beating, he thought back to ninth grade English class. He and Heather had sat together and really had some fun conversations. He hoped she would still remember that. He hadn't been seated by her in a class this year and was too shy to do anything more than smile and nod when he had seen her in the hall. The last few times she hadn't seemed to notice him but that was probably due to her friends keeping her distracted.

Nick let out a sigh of relief as Def Leppard rang out, filling the commons area with cheers. Of course, this meant he would need to wait a bit longer but he would have more time to plan his move.

"So, are you going to ask anyone to dance?" Oscar's question finally grabbed his attention.

"I don't know. Maybe for a slow dance...I'm not that good at fast-dancing." Nick felt like this was the understatement of a lifetime but was relieved that Oscar didn't dig into him.

"Fast-dancing is easy. All you have to do is pretend like you're boxing and move around the dance floor."

Nick withheld a snicker as he watched Oscar shuffle around in his seat. His focus abruptly changed as he saw Heather walking across the room.

"Who are you looking at?" Oscar asked, noting Nick's sudden mental departure.

"Nobody," he replied, trying to avoid being caught staring as he looked away a moment too late to preclude Oscar from following his gaze.

"You were checking out Heather, weren't you?"

Nick's heart leapt. Did Oscar know that he liked Heather? He would have to cover his tracks. "No, I just know her from junior high, that's all. That doesn't mean I was checking her out."

"You don't know her."

Why did Oscar have to be like this? Why did he have to start an argument, especially where people could hear?

"Yes, I do. I used to sit by her in English class."

"But you never talked to her."

"Of course I did."

"So, why don't you ask her to dance?"

"You think I won't?"

"I know you won't. You're not capable. You'll freeze up before you make it half way across the floor."

Nick was so angry with Oscar that he thought he was going to explode. He was glad that there was loud music to cover his shouting.

"Don't ever tell me that I can't do something! I'll ask her, I'm just going to wait for a slow song, that's all."

With that, Nick turned his back to Oscar. The gauntlet had been thrown down and he had accepted the challenge. He suddenly felt sick. He knew that he was going to have to go through with this. Maybe he would get lucky and she would leave before another slow song was played? Nick pondered such scenarios as he nervously looked around the commons.

In the distance, Dino caught Nick's eye. He was talking to Cheri Winters, the beautiful blonde cheerleader that Nick knew Dino liked. The big guy was apparently asking her to dance. Nick thought back to cutting weight for his first match and remembered Dino talking about Cheri and mentioning that she worked at A'Romano's. Nick never thought the big guy would make such a bold move. "When I'm a state champ, I'll be able to dance with anyone I want," thought Nick. "Look at Dino over there talking to the most beautiful girl in the school."

Nick was surprised to see Cheri make some gestures, causing Dino to walk away. However, he was glad as the big guy walked over to him and Oscar. It would be nice to have some civil company.

Before Nick could greet his friend, the familiar voice of Joel Vassec echoed in his ears. "You guys should be out there dancing. You could use the extra movement to lose a few pounds." The senior then turned his attention to Dino, asking if he had just asked Cheri to dance.

"Yeah, but she and her friends are leaving so she couldn't," Dino replied.

"It doesn't look like they're leaving to me." Joel responded, nodding over to where Cheri and her friends were still having a good time, looking over toward the foursome of wrestlers and talking and giggling among themselves.

"She's a tease," Joel continued. "She wants me but I wouldn't ever waste my time on a tease like her."

"She is not, she's really nice," Dino countered.

"Whatever, Benzy, you're just whipped because she's hot."

As a girl grabbed Vassec and led him toward the dance floor, the senior commented over his shoulder, "Gotta go, losers."

Nick was not the least bit sad to see him go. Unfortunately, his delight in seeing Joel walk away was replaced with terror as the DJ switched to a slow song.

"This is it, Castle, time for you to show your stuff." Oscar's words rang in Nick's ears. He wondered if he could possibly look as pale and sickly as he felt. Reluctantly, he got to his feet and pushed in his chair.

"What's up?" Dino inquired.

"Castle is going to ask someone to dance. Actually, he isn't but he's just too afraid to admit it."

"Oh, yeah?" was all that Nick could muster as he started walking across the room. He was petrified. Was his breath all right? How would he ask her?

Cheri Winters passed him and he was surprised to see her walk up and ask Dino to dance, an offer that was immediately accepted. Maybe there was hope for Dino and Cheri after all. If that could work, surely Nick could get someone to dance with him.

The space between Nick and Heather seemed like the length of a basketball court as the boy made his way to where she stood. He felt like a spotlight was on him and that every person along the way was looking at him, watching to see what he was going to do. Heather was watching him too as he neared. He tried to look confident but still stumbled over his words.

"Hi, Heather. Would you…would you like to dance…with me?" The words seemed choppy and contrived. He felt his face turning beet red as he stood there, listening to her friends giggle, waiting for what seemed like an eternity before she answered.

"No."

One of the shortest words in the English vocabulary hit Nick like a truck full of bricks. The girl punctuated her answer by turning back to her friends with an almost 'offended' look on her face.

"Oh, okay," was all that Nick could stammer as he turned back the way he came, the loud giggling of Heather's friends still ringing in his ears. The distance between Nick's original seat and his current location near Heather seemed to have expanded to at least the length of a football field. He felt completely ashamed as he walked back, trying not to make eye contact with anyone who had seen him get rejected, a number which he was sure was in the hundreds and included everyone in the room.

Nick noted that Oscar was not at their table. Apparently he was out dancing, making Nick the lone figure who had been turned down. As if being discarded wasn't enough, he would now have to go back and sit by himself, thus fulfilling the role of 'loser' that he seemed to be playing so well right now. Turning a brighter shade of red, he asked himself how his plight could possibly get any worse.

He immediately regretted asking himself the question as he lost his balance and the floor suddenly rose to meet him. Laughter again rang in his ears as the realization hit him that it wasn't his own volition which had brought him to this position but a well-placed foot of Todd Johnson that had kicked out and tripped him.

"No wonder nobody wants to dance with you, Cass-hole, look how clumsy you are." Yelling over to Tom Mack, Todd continued, "Mack, you must really suck if you can't even beat clumsy Cass-hole."

Nick was completely jittery. It took him a fraction of a second to decide that he had absorbed all the humiliation that he could take. He no longer cared about what was going to happen to him. They could suspend him from school, kick him off the team, put him in detention, it didn't matter. He jumped to his feet ready to take a swing at the larger boy, his cronies and whoever else wanted a piece of him.

He trembled as he rose, fists clenched, fighting the overwhelming emotions that made him want to explode, cry and completely destroy everything and everyone around him.

"Back off Castle, I'll take care of this." The voice was that of Mr. McNeely, Nick's Gym teacher, who had somehow stepped between the two boys, causing Nick to fall back. "I saw that, Mr. Johnson. I heard what you said too. I'm not going to tolerate that kind of behavior or that kind of language at this dance. Let's go to visit the principal, shall we?"

Nick was so far beyond livid that he could not fathom what he should do. He had been given a single chance to step up and show that he was not a coward and his Gym teacher had ruined it. He trembled as he watched Mr. McNeely lead Todd away. Not knowing what else he could possibly do, Nick walked toward the water fountain, wishing that he could somehow find a way to wash himself down the drain to a place where nobody could see him and, more importantly, a place where nobody knew him.

Chapter 23

The chill ran down Nick's spine as he moved the bar on the scale. He let it rest on 135 pounds and put both of his arms down by his sides. "Please let it break," he pleaded to no avail. The bracket sat firmly against the top of the metal housing, indicating that he was still over weight.

Nick felt sick. He had been wrestling so well lately at practice. He just wanted to get on the mat and prove himself tonight. He knew he could beat this kid.

He moved the bar an eighth of a pound to the right but it did not change the bracket's position.

He was tired, almost too tired to move, but he would have to keep going. He moved the bar another eighth pound and held his breath as he watched the tiny crack of space appear between the bracket and the housing.

"A quarter pound," he thought. That wasn't so bad, was it? He still had a good half an hour until weigh-in. He scurried to don a tee shirt, sweatshirt, jacket and sweat pants. Pulling on his gloves and stocking cap, he briefly pondered how he would look without hair. Shaving his head would cut a good eighth of a pound, right?

Slipping his shoes on, Nick sprinted out of the locker room and up the stairs to the wrestling room. Dino had been on weight this week so Nick was the only fat guy on the team. He refused to let his team down, especially when the opposing team's 135-pound wrestler was one of the few wrestlers Nick could think of that was struggling even more than Nick.

Nick had seen the guy at the dual tournament a week and a half earlier. He had looked like a fish, flopping around on the mat prior to being pinned. Nick relished that he would have the chance to secure this win tonight to get himself back on track. He grabbed a jump rope and began sprinting in place. He needed to get a sweat going quickly and keep it going as long as possible. He amazed himself at how rapidly he got to a hundred rotations.

Fifteen minutes later, Nick's muscles cried out in agony. He could not believe how tired he felt but he could feel the moisture leaving his pores in line with the energy leaving his body. He wanted to lie down and either sleep or die. At this point, it really didn't matter to Nick which his body chose. What mattered was that his body, which was screaming for some kind of nourishment, would finally be getting well deserved rest.

This rest was not meant to be. Nick watched as Coach Granger reached the top of the stairs. Instead of lying down, the boy picked up his pace even further although he was sure that he was quickly reaching official dehydration. He didn't need a lecture from his coach on the finer points of weight cutting.

"You are still over?" the grouchy man barked as he drew near.

"Less than a quarter pound," Nick replied, continuing his workout. "I can run it off."

Granger used a few choice curse words to get his point across. "No, it's too late, the other team is here. We're going with Mack, he just weighed in at 133."

Nick couldn't believe his ears. They were going to cut him? After all that he had been through? He began to protest but was immediately cut off by his coach.

"You make weight, you wrestle. You don't show up for weigh-in a quarter pound over and expect to be allowed some leeway. Go downstairs and give your varsity uniform to Mack. We'll see if we can get you a JV match at 140 pounds."

Nick was approaching the stage of delirium. On one hand, he wanted to jump on his coach and beat the man to a bloody pulp. At the same time, he wanted to curl up in a ball and die. In the end, he did neither. He made the labored journey down the stairs to turn over his uniform.

Chapter 24

I must have been made to suffer," Nick thought as he watched Tom Mack being taken down. The older boy had a big smile on his face as the foghorn sounded and the stands erupted with cheering. Tom got up, shook hands with his opponent, and having dominated most of the match, had his hand raised in victory.

Nick sat in the stands with his dad and brother, dreading the pending conversation. Nick had beaten a 145-pound wrestler in an exhibition match before the dual. Unfortunately, nobody had been there to see the match.

"You could have beaten that kid," Ron commented.

Nick didn't even reply. All conversation with Ron this evening had centered around Nick's lack of varsity wins, how Nick wrestled like a champion at practice but not when it counted, and how having only one win in seven varsity matches was completely unacceptable. Their dad had stepped in more than once to stop his sons from arguing.

Nick was tired. He was physically tired, tired of his brother's negative comments and tired of his coach. All Nick would have needed was another fifteen minutes of jumping rope and running. His coach had stolen a varsity win from Nick by not waiting a measly fifteen extra minutes. This was the fact he dwelled on while watching the next six matches, combinations of wins and losses that left Riverside down by six points going into Dino's match.

Nick knew that it was unlikely his team would win tonight. To do so would require Dino to pin one of the top wrestlers in the state and Clifford Vassec to win his heavyweight match, something the large boy had yet to do this season.

Nick's mind again went back to the 135-pound match. If he had wrestled tonight, he was sure that he could have come out with a pin or a major decision, giving his team more points than Tom Mack had. His face was locked in a snarl as he watched Dino manhandling his opponent.

"This guy is ranked fourth in the state? He doesn't look that good," Nick commented to his brother.

"That's because Benzy is an animal," his brother replied.

Neither boy looked at the other as they discussed the match. Their eyes were locked on Dino as he slowly circled Danny Crissler, his opponent.

Already down seven points, Crissler tried to muscle in on Dino to set him up for a head and arm throw. With surprising quickness for a kid his size, Dino stepped to the side, popped his hips and launched his opponent, throwing the large boy straight to his back.

As Crissler scrambled to his belly, Dino gained leverage on top of him; put both legs in and began cranking on a half nelson. Crissler's pain showed clearly on his face as Dino added pressure to the boy's neck and shoulder but didn't let him turn.

"Just pin him Benzy, we need the points," Ron muttered. He and his brother both knew that Dino would eventually turn his opponent to his back but that he would hold him in pain for several more seconds, sending the message that he was not someone to mess with.

"The big guy is indestructible," thought Nick as Dino finally allowed Crissler to turn to his back, ending his pain and concluding the match with a pin.

Chapter 25

Sean studied Cole Tyler from across the room, wondering about the contents of the notes on his scratch pad. As Riverside had lost 27 to 33, his only hope was that the man had found redeeming qualities in a few of his wrestlers. He jogged across the gym and barely caught the man before he made his way out the door.

"What did you think?" Sean inquired.

"Maybe two of your kids have promise. Your seniors are welcome at our practice on the 28th. Your young guys wouldn't make a decent meal for the University wrestlers."

"What about Benz?"

Cole looked annoyed, as if he was about to kick himself for not leaving early.

"He's a strong kid, I'll give him that, but he doesn't look like he's done growing. If he wrestled for us, it would be at heavyweight. Bota from Jamestown has already committed to us. He's an ox 70 pounds bigger than Benz. He's going to be our man once our current heavyweight graduates."

Sean was disappointed at the man's comments. Surely there could be some kind of spot for a wrestler as dominant as Benz. He regained hope as Cole stopped and turned with an inquisitive look on his face.

"Do you have any western conference teams coming here this year?" the man asked.

"No," Sean responded, not quite understanding the tangent subject.

"There is a kid named Spegidos that wrestles 130 for one of the schools up in the northwestern corner. Let me know how he looks if you see him at any tournaments. He's supposed to be phenomenal. Nobody has lasted the entire six minutes with him this season."

Sean knew exactly who Cole was talking about and didn't know whether to be offended that his own wrestlers were being overlooked or honored to be an unofficial scout for the university. He registered a note in his mind to watch for Spegidos at the upcoming holiday tournament. Staying in Cole's good graces certainly couldn't hurt as he continued to look for ways to get Dino noticed.

Chapter 26

Nick's mind was on his day ahead as he cleaned the breakfast dishes, taking a break from time to time to look out the window at the snow accumulating in the yard. It had been bitterly cold as he and Chewie had completed his paper route, giving the boy extra incentive to deliver the papers quickly and get back inside.

A dozen subjects ricocheted around in his head. Should he have eaten so much this morning? Would he have to wrestle off to get his varsity spot back? Could he avoid Todd Johnson in Biology class somehow? Should he ever talk to Heather again? All of these subjects added more stress to Nick's life than he really needed. He was so wound up that the sudden explosion of cursing by his brother made Nick jump a good six inches.

"What?" Nick questioned, suddenly feeling defensive.

"How can you deliver this garbage?" the older boy questioned, pointing at the newspaper. "Look at this crap!"

Nick had no idea what his brother was talking about but didn't have a chance to reply before Ron continued his tirade, reading from an article in the sports section.

"Former Riverside stand-out, Ron Castle, cheers his team on from the sidelines during the team's 27 – 33 dual loss Tuesday evening."

He crumpled the paper and threw it across the room.

"I'm so sick of it!!!" the boy yelled, adding a few profanities to ensure that his point came across. "I pinned my way through the conference tournament last year and was lucky to be noted in the box scores. Now, because I'm a cripple, I'm suddenly front-page news!!!"

Nick stood back as he watched his father come storming into the room.

"Ron, you watch your language!" the man demanded. "You're not too old to have your mouth washed out with soap. If your mother hadn't already left for work, she'd be filling your chops with Irish Spring."

"But Dad…" the older boy began to complain before being completely cut off by his father.

"I know it's not what you would like but deal with it!"

Mr. Castle grabbed the crumpled paper from the floor and looked at the offending page.

"Hard luck stories sell," he continued. "If they are going to print your picture to move a few more newspapers, so be it. It doesn't have to ruin your day and it certainly doesn't have to create a reason for the rest of us to listen to a string of profanity. 'FORMER Riverside stand-out' is a bunch of garbage. If they had any idea the work you put in at the rehab, their jaws would drop in awe. Unfortunately, that isn't news that sells so we're going to have to deal with life as it is for the time being."

Mr. Castle crossed the room and looked briefly out the window.

"You're a champ, son," he said to Ron.

Then, turning to Nick, he continued, "Both of you are. No matter what happens, I'll always be proud of both of you."

Nick was glad that, despite everything else going on, he knew he could count on his dad's support. He just wished that he could count on the same support at school.

Chapter 27

Nick and Dino talked as they headed toward the locker room. Nick was worn down physically but was excited about how well he had matched up with Bradford, a senior, at today's practice during their final live match. The boy was one weight class, five pounds, heavier than Nick but Nick had stayed with him the entire match, losing by a mere point.

Nick was glad to have Dino's ear for a minute. He had been meaning to compliment the big guy on his dominating victory from the prior night.

"That kid you wrestled isn't going to be able to turn his head for a month," the smaller wrestler commented.

Dino smiled wryly, savoring the memory. "He ought to know that if he's going to mess with the big dog, he's going to get hurt. I like to put in both legs and crank on guys like that sometimes and not let them turn. It's just a reminder that they're not as indestructible as they think they are."

The words were still ringing in Nick's ears when the two boys passed the coaches' office. Nick was still waiting for his opportunity to prove that some people weren't as indestructible as they think they are. He was confident that his time would come.

"Castle! I need to have a word with you," Coach Granger's voice echoed from the office.

Nick looked at Dino tensely. The older boy only met Nick's gaze as he patted the boy on the back and nodded, before turning to make his way toward the student locker room.

"What does he want now?" was Nick's only thought as he approached his coach. His adrenaline started to flow, making some of his physical weariness seem to subside.

"Nick, have a seat," the man directed.

Nick did as he was told. He was nervous as he never knew what to expect from this man anymore. He hoped that this meeting would be short and not make his situation any more precarious. He imagined that he was about to be told that he would need to do some special training to keep his weight down or that Granger was going to personally weigh him in daily to ensure that Nick was close to 135 pounds.

What Granger revealed was far worse than a plan to micromanage Nick and his weight. The boy felt his hands grip the arms of the chair as the coach decreed, "Nick, I have decided that Mack will be our 135-pounder at the pre-Christmas tournament."

Nick's blood began to boil as he protested, "I beat him in the wrestle-off!"

Cutting him off, the coach retaliated, "Regardless of that fact, he proved himself in this week's dual. Until you can prove to me that you should be varsity, we go with him."

Nick felt himself getting red as tears of anger welled in his eyes.

"It isn't fair," the boy continued. "I beat him twice in wrestle-offs, I beat that 145-pounder last night. I…"

His coach cut him off. "This isn't a democracy, until I decide otherwise, he's in. You will be junior varsity for now."

Nick began to protest again but a stern look from Granger made it obvious that the conversation was over. The boy jumped out of his chair. He wanted to get out of that office as soon as possible. He wheeled around, almost running into Coach MacCallister who had just entered the office behind him.

"Hey Castle..." Sean started but Nick was already past him, racing out the door.

Startled by Nick's erratic behavior, Sean asked Granger the obvious question of what was wrong with Nick.

"Mack is our man," the head coach informed him, "unless Castle someday decides that he's going to wrestle when it counts like he does in practice."

Sean could only nod in acknowledgement as he searched for a way to shed positive light on Nick.

"The thing is, he's obviously got the tools to win," Sean started, pleading Nick's case. "He beat that kid last night and he was giving up almost ten pounds. I don't know if he's just lacking the confidence to be varsity or if he's wearing himself out cutting weight but, you have to admit, the kid has potential."

Granger shifted his eyes away from Sean. Despite his rough demeanor, it appeared that he wasn't comfortable having this confrontation with his assistant coach.

"Once he starts living up to that potential," the head coach rebutted, "he's welcome back in the varsity line-up. Until then, Mack is at 135."

Sean studied the man, wondering why he was so out of sorts.

"I had his brother to contend with last year," Granger continued. "The kid was an arrogant jerk on and off the mat but for the most part, during his matches, he could do no wrong. You could almost always count on a win. This one can't seem to do anything right. He can't make weight, when he does, he doesn't win…"

"He has a lot of heart," Sean cut in. "You've seen him at practice. He shows up early and never misses practice, not even the optional sessions. He goes at top speed the entire time and then runs extra afterward. He'll come around."

"Not before this weekend's tournament, he won't."

Sean tried to continue but Granger cut him off.

"Do you have any thoughts on how to keep Benz's weight down for this weekend?"

The abrupt change in topic made it clear to Sean that the discussion about Nick was over for now. Sean would be sure to refine his talking points before their next round. He wasn't going to give up on Nick without a fight.

"I've got that special practice Thursday morning for fat guys," Sean answered. "Dino will be there. He hasn't missed yet. I've already told him I'll take him to work out at the dome early Friday morning before weigh-in if necessary. There is enough room in that facility for him to run ten different ways to make weight. Trust me, he'll be 215 pounds or lighter when he steps on the scale."

Granger grumbled something under his breath before turning back to Sean.

"One other thing," the older man concluded. "I want Hermanns and Bradford to wrestle Castle these next few days. Feel free to pair Mack with anyone but Castle. If I see the two of them pounding it out at any time this week, I'll have your hide tanned and displayed on this office wall."

Sean pondered whether or not he should point out the fact that a tanned hide could only improve the office's appearance. Thinking better of further agitating the man, he simply nodded his acceptance of the orders and walked out.

Chapter 28

Nick lay quietly on his bed, listening to his music and staring at the ceiling. He was so angry that he felt like he might combust. His coach had robbed him! How could he ever trust the man again when he had so flagrantly violated both the protocol of the sport and the trust of one of his most dedicated wrestlers?

Nick wanted to punch someone. In particular, he wanted to punch his coach. He knew that doing so would get him kicked off the team but, at this point, there wasn't much incentive to stay. He heard the click of the door, but refused to acknowledge his father as the man entered. There was nothing the man could say right now that could make him feel any better.

"Are you going to be all right?" his father asked.

"Yeah," Nick lied. His whole reason for existence had just been stripped away from him. How could he possibly be all right any time in the near future? As if he didn't have enough problems trying to meet girls, this would make things worse. Nick didn't even want to think about how Todd Johnson could use this in ridiculing him. Things were certainly not going to be all right.

"Ronnie says you've been temporarily moved down."

Nick didn't have to ask how Ron knew. Joel Vassec had undoubtedly called him in a moment of gleeful joy to inform Nick's older brother that Nick had been downgraded. If Nick was going to punch his coach and get kicked off of the team, he may as well take the next step and punch Vassec on his way out the door.

Lost in his own thoughts, it didn't register with Nick that he had never responded to his father.

"Would you like to talk about it?"

Nick finally turned to face the man. "It's not fair! I've beaten him twice!" the boy exclaimed. He didn't need to go into details with his dad. The senior Castle knew the rules of the wrestling room. Why didn't Coach Granger?

"I know, kid," the man replied softly.

Nick got up and walked away from his dad, toward the window, fuming as he paced the room. He didn't want the man to see the anger in his face or puffiness from the tears that he had been holding back.

"I won the wrestle-off so I'm varsity. He lost so he's JV. That is how it works. Granger can't change the rules mid-stream. It's not fair! How can he expect anyone on the team to follow him if he isn't going to follow his own rules? Those rules have always been in place."

He turned around in his circuit and ran head-long into his father, smacking his forehead into the big man's chest. Before he cared to move, he felt his father's large arms clasp behind his back, catching the boy in a big hug.

There was nothing that Nick's dad could say to make the situation better. But somehow, having him there seemed to make all of the difference in the world that night.

Chapter 29

She was cute," Sean thought as the woman walked away. He would have to remember that her name was Cindy next time he saw her on campus. Since he was sober at this concert, remembering her name did not seem like nearly as difficult a task as it would have been in a similar situation a year earlier, during his drinking days.

The young man looked around the room to see the status of the Beta Beta Beta brothers he had driven to the event. He could see Darrel Zok talking to a woman who did not look the least bit interested. Sean was not surprised as Darrel's attempts to pick up women usually ended with the woman walking away in a huff, Darrel getting slapped, Darrel getting a face full of beer, or all three. This particular woman was twirling her hair, giving the signal to one of her friends to rescue her from talking to the obnoxious young man. Sean felt good that this woman would not completely destroy Darrel's confidence.

Sean watched the beer flowing and suddenly felt very proud of his accomplishment over the past six months. Kelly and others had been very supportive of Sean's alcohol avoidance at first but, over time, Kelly in particular seemed to miss having Sean as his primary drinking buddy. Sean's position as perpetual designated driver seemed to help but he could tell that Kelly really missed the old days and the chaos they had created.

Sean couldn't locate anyone else from his group but was sure that all three were somewhere in the crowd, drinking heavily and trying to make inroads with members of the opposite sex. As he panned the crowd, his gaze fell upon the person whom he least wanted to see, Mandi Isacson. His blood froze as he realized that, not only was she in the room, she seemed to have noticed him and was moving through the crowd in his direction.

Looking for an escape route, Sean casually turned and began walking away from her. He was amazed at how the crowd seemed to bunch up exactly where he needed to walk. "Look natural," he thought as he tried to gently make his way between people and find a way to disappear from her radar. To his chagrin, the crowd seemed to be largely moving against his flow, approaching the stage as the band prepared for its final number.

"Hey Mac!" The voice was unmistakable and right behind him. He felt her hand on his shoulder and knew that it was too late for him to get away.

"Be polite." The words appeared in his mind as he made a concerted effort to keep his composure. He felt unusually awkward and nervous. Hoping that this didn't show, Sean turned to face the woman who had most recently broken his heart.

"Hey Mandi, I was just going," Sean explained.

"Have you seen Ted Graham?" she asked. "He was supposed to meet me by the bar but I didn't see him there."

She was slurring her words and was clearly liquored. He could not believe that she would have the audacity to approach him and ask him for directions to another man. Was she trying to torture him?

What made things worse was the man she was looking for. Sean couldn't say he knew Ted Graham very well. Their paths had crossed a time or two at bars and parties. Ted exemplified everything that Sean wasn't. He was tall and Adonis-like good looking. His clothes and hair were always impeccable and he always had women fawning over him. Was he the one that Mandi had chosen over Sean a month and a half earlier?

"I saw him closer to the stage earlier tonight," was Sean's only reply as he pointed to the stage at the other end of the room. The statement was as true as it would have been two hours earlier; it just wouldn't necessarily get Mandi to Ted at this point in the evening.

"Did you ever get those pictures from the homecoming banquet? That was a fun night."

The change in subject to that of their one and only date caught Sean off guard.

"I think they came in last week," he replied.

This was more of a lie than his prior stretch of the truth. Sean knew full well that the pictures had arrived. As soon as the homecoming chairman had handed him the envelope, Sean had tossed it in a drawer for future burning.

"Can I get mine?"

Sean was taken aback at the fact that Mandi would want those pictures given the way that the night had ended. Did they contain good memories for her? If so, he certainly couldn't echo her sentiments. How was he going to get out of this conversation but still remain polite? A standard delay tactic was in order.

"Yeah, can I call and get your mailing address tomorrow?" he asked.

"No, just bring them by. I'll be around tomorrow night."

Before Sean could manage a reply, Mandi located Ted and began walking away. Ted was halfway across the room and completely inebriated. As usual, he had a couple of women hanging around him.

Mandi didn't even look toward Sean as she waved goodbye and yelled, "There he is. See you tomorrow, Mac."

As Sean watched her go, it became clear to him that he had once again been 'Mandied' as he called it. Despite his best laid plans, he now felt obligated to drive all the way across town and deliver a set of pictures to her that he himself didn't want to look at. He wished that he had burned them. The whole situation gave him a headache as he looked around for his buddies.

Chapter 30

Nick sat in the locker room, slowly getting dressed. Practice had been fine yet, for whatever reason, he was feeling sluggish again. Whether he wanted to admit it or not, having to sit out of the pre-Christmas tournament was taking a toll on his morale.

He watched Dino walk over to the scale, step on and grimace. For the first time ever, he wished that he had to cut weight. The misery was fine if it led to the prize. Right now, Nick didn't even have a prize to chase. There was no state title for junior varsity. Being first among those on the second string wasn't something that the state deemed to be worth celebrating.

Dino crossed back near Nick's bench and started getting dressed. He looked as down as Nick felt. Maybe he needed an encouraging word.

"Are you close to your weight?" Nick asked.

"Five pounds under," Dino replied with a tired, wry smile.

Nick was amazed that Dino could appear so defeated on the scale when he had the opportunity to eat like a horse for the next few days before the tournament. This was truly someone that Nick wanted to emulate.

"Really?" was all the boy could respond.

"Yes," Dino continued, "if I want to weigh in as a Sumo wrestler."

Nick shook his head and smiled at Dino's wit. He couldn't believe that he had been caught by the bigger boy's unusual sense of humor. Still, for whatever reason, it made him feel a little better as he donned his jacket, mittens and cap and headed out into the night.

Chapter 31

Sean sat in his Galaxie 500, staring at the photos in front of him. He dreaded getting out of the car, not so much for the sub-zero temperatures he would face but more the thought of his destination. Parked in the parking lot of Mandi's apartment building, Sean was a couple of dozen paces from the hallway that held one of his worst recent memories.

Sean coughed. His throat was starting to get sore, the usual early sign of the onset of the flu. The good news was that he would be able to get home, drink lots of water and get to bed early. The best way to avoid the flu was to nip it in the bud. If all else failed, perhaps he could use the forthcoming illness as a reason to leave right away.

To stall away a bit more time, Sean opened the envelope. As he poured the pictures into his hand, he quickly realized that looking at them was a mistake. Out of all of Sean's bad relationships, this may have been the worst. It was certainly the one that was most fresh in his mind. Looking through the pictures, his heart began to beat rapidly. There she was; sitting on his lap in one, dancing with him in another and holding out a beer in the third with that painfully beautiful smile of hers. He wanted to hate her. He thought he did. He certainly did when she wasn't around. Now he wasn't quite sure.

As he looked at the picture of the two of them dancing, he wanted to hold her like that again. He remembered holding her close and smelling her hair. What was it about her that made her fit so well in his arms?

He shook his head and made himself look away but there was no escaping the memories of that night. His gaze fell on the entrance door of her apartment building. "See, I can open doors myself," she had proclaimed that night as she walked into the building.

It was clearly a reference to the fact that he had opened every single door for her, with the exception of the ladies' room door, over the prior several hours. She was cute, feisty and independent. All three drove him wild.

He remembered the walk to her apartment door as she went on and on about how fun the night had been and that they didn't go out like that nearly enough. He had wanted to say that he had every night for the rest of his life free and that she could pick any or all of them. In fact, he probably did. Details about his half of the dialog were far less clear than hers. As she unlocked the door, he unwrapped her from his coat. The hair stood up on his neck as he anticipated the moment.

She turned back to face him and he leaned in to kiss her. The following several seconds would be burned in his mind forever.

"What are you doing?" she had asked.

Sean had frozen as if she had just shot him with a tazer. Had he misread her cues? He certainly wasn't going to force himself on her. Did she think that he was going to try something completely inappropriate? This would seem to be the case given the way she cringed and stepped backward.

"I just thought I'd give you a goodnight kiss," Sean had responded, not knowing what else he could possibly say.

"I don't think my boyfriend would appreciate that," was her only reply as she stepped backward into the apartment and shut the door.

Sean had mouthed the word, 'boyfriend?' that night as he stood there looking like a fool. The memory of the scene made him mouth the word again as he stood outside that same door holding Mandi's pictures. How could she have accepted a date with him if she had a boyfriend? Why had she not mentioned said boyfriend anytime during the several weeks preceding the homecoming banquet? How could he have let himself fall so hard for someone, not even knowing that she was already in a relationship?

Sean turned to walk away. He didn't want to knock on the door, despite the fact that he had driven across town to deliver the pictures. He didn't want to see her. He didn't want to talk to her. He didn't want to give her any kind of opportunity to tear his guts out like she had that night.

Taking a deep breath, Sean turned back. He would do this thing. He had told her that he would bring the pictures over tonight and that is what he intended to do. "Hello, here are your pictures, I've got to go." Sean rehearsed the line in his head.

He knocked on the door and waited. Nothing happened. There was no sound from within. He knocked again. The anger started welling up in him. He had driven all the way across town to deliver pictures to someone that he didn't want to see and she had the audacity to stand him up? It was completely unbelievable to him. How can a human being do that to another human being? Sean wanted to tear the pictures apart and leave them in a pile in front of her door. Better yet, he wanted to burn them and use the ashes to write some nasty message on that demonic door that he now stared at like an idiot, once again. How could she do this?

Sean needed to get out and he needed to get out now. He bent down, shoved the envelope under the door, turned and walked away feeling that steam must be resonating from his scalp as he marched away. If he ever saw her again, he would ignore her. If he could think of something better, he would do that too. For now, ignoring her was a good start. If he had his way, he would never see her again, which was the thought echoing through his mind when he heard the click.

"Hello?" the small voice sounded from behind him.

Sean stopped in his tracks and his heart sank. Was that her? Had she been there all along? Was he going to have to see her? He turned around to face the voice and found Mandi, standing in her doorway in an old tee shirt and sweat pants. Her short black hair was a mess; the little make-up that she wore was running down her cheeks, the unmistakable tracks of tears. To most people, she would have looked like a complete disaster. To Sean, she was the world's most beautiful woman. His heart dropped again as he returned to talk to her.

Chapter 32

Oh, you are home. I brought those pictures," Sean said as he approached Mandi.

Mandi opened the door a little further. She saw the envelope on the floor but it didn't seem to register that the envelope had anything to do with Sean's prior sentence.

"Mac, I didn't know it was you. I didn't know that you were coming over."

The comment caught Sean a bit off guard. He had spent nearly 24 hours dreading this moment. How could she have not even remembered asking him to come over? He would have been hurt if he had not been so concerned about her present state.

"Are you all right?" he inquired as he approached.

"I've just had a rough night. Do you want to come in?"

Sean was stunned and torn. He had hoped to just drop off the pictures and leave. But now, she seemed so sad, so helpless. What was wrong? Was she all right? He didn't want to get too close but at the same time, he couldn't resist the chance to spend time with her.

"Yeah...okay...but I can't stay long." he stammered. "I've got to study for a test I have tomorrow." He hoped that the latter excuse would help get him out of her apartment if he got too uncomfortable.

As he entered the apartment, he couldn't help but think that it looked as torn up as Mandi did. Papers were scattered all over the floor. Food, dishes and cooking utensils were piled up in the kitchen and a bottle of Blue Hawaiian sat on the table, nearly empty.

"Do you want a drink?" she offered, motioning toward the bottle.

"No thanks," he replied. Perhaps she had forgotten that he no longer drank? Maybe it was a symptom of whatever she was dealing with that night? He couldn't be sure.

"Good, it leaves more for me," she retorted, taking another swig from the bottle and nearly losing her balance.

Sean was getting very concerned about her lack of coherence.

"How much have you had to drink?" he asked.

Mandi tried to focus as she stared bleary-eyed at the bottle.

"This and two beers."

It was a substantial amount of alcohol for a person of her size. Sean had seen her hold her booze in several nights of partying but this night's consumption seemed way over the top, especially considering it wasn't even 8:00. He began to feel uneasy.

"Is something wrong?" he finally asked.

"Of course something's wrong, idiot!" she yelled back at him.

The angry reply caught Sean off guard. He stood helplessly and watched as Mandi fell to the couch and resumed her crying.

Not knowing what else to do, Sean moved right in front of Mandi, kneeling in front of the couch, putting his hand gently on the young woman's shoulder as he asked if she wanted to talk.

He didn't have to wait for a reply as Mandi immediately launched into her story. The stream of tears was constant as she relayed that she and Ted Graham were supposed to have a date that night. When she went to his house to pick him up, he didn't come to the door so she walked in to find him escorting some other woman to his bedroom.

"Hey, now's not a good time," was all that Ted had said to her as he walked into the bedroom and shut the door.

The story didn't improve Ted's standing in Sean's mind. He had always considered the man to be the "love 'em and leave 'em" type and this certainly confirmed his suspicion. He didn't know whether his feelings were more of anger toward Ted or sorrow for Mandi.

Mandi's crying continued as she pushed her face into Sean's shoulder and pounded hard on his chest. Then, suddenly, she turned completely pale and her eyes rolled momentarily.

Sean's heart pounded as he watched her eyes drift back to focus on him.

"I don't want to puke," she said and immediately hurled on the couch, herself, the floor and Sean's pants and foot.

Sean looked around frantically as Mandi continued to heave. Finding a potato chip bag, he quickly dumped its contents onto the coffee table and handed the bag to Mandi so that she could vomit into it.

The vomit was soon nearly everywhere. Knowing from vast experience how uncomfortable Mandi had to be, Sean excused himself to the bathroom to find her some towels and, hopefully, a damp wash cloth.

Flipping on the light to the bathroom, Sean was pleased to find a set of towels which looked clean. It was a small victory that lifted his heart. He stepped carefully across the floor, attempting to stay on the tile portion and avoid stepping on Mandi's bright white rugs with his vomit-covered shoes. To no avail, a small red disc dropped from his pants cuff onto one of the rugs. As he stooped to pick it off, he noticed a few other similar dots on his shoe.

"What has she been eating?" the young man wondered as he examined the small object. His blood suddenly ran cold as he raised his eyes to the vanity top and noticed half a dozen empty pill containers scattered across it.

Sean blurted out a few abrupt curses as he grabbed the bathroom garbage can and ran back to the living room where Mandi was now passed out on the couch.

Terrified, the young man screamed, "No!" as he grabbed her limp body and stuck his fingers down her throat. Mandi's arms flailed as her body temporarily fought the urge to vomit and she began dry-heaving.

"Don't go to sleep on me!" Sean yelled. "Do not go to sleep!"

Mandi looked up at him, completely dazed, as Sean picked her off the couch and half-carried, half-dragged her to the kitchen.

"Come on, work with me!" he commanded as he tried to get her to fight her body's attempts to shut down and lose consciousness.

Finding her telephone, Sean dialed with one hand as he held her up with his other arm.

"I need an ambulance NOW!!!" he shouted into the receiver.

Chapter 33

Sean had never been to an emergency room sober and conscious before that night. Noting the chaos, he hoped that this would be his first and last time. He looked anxiously past the nurse toward the room into which they had wheeled Mandi. He didn't have time for the questions. He just wanted to know that Mandi was out of danger.

"I don't know," he replied to her latest question. "She took some pills…a bunch of them. The bottles are all over the sink in her bathroom."

"What time did she take them?"

Sean felt like he was being shaken down by the police. "I don't know! I wasn't there! Is she going be all right?"

"About what time did she take them?" the nurse continued, ignoring Sean's question. "We need this information so that we can get her the proper treatment."

Sean's mind raced. "Around 7:00, maybe?" he finally answered.

He noted that the clock on the ER wall read only 8:35 and was amazed that the events of this evening could have all been squeezed into an hour. It seemed like it had been at least a week since he had first knocked on her door.

"The doctor will be out shortly," the nurse stated calmly as she turned and walked away.

Sean found a seat and waited for what seemed like an eternity. He switched off between reading irrelevant magazines and watching meaningless TV for nearly two hours before a doctor finally approached him.

"Are you the young man who brought Miss Isacson in?" the doctor inquired.

Sean replied affirmatively, anxious to finally be talking to someone who would have answers.

"She seems to have had quite a night. Do you want to tell me about it?" The doctor's question seemed more like an accusation.

"She took some pills and drank some beer and schnapps."

The doctor glared at Sean as he continued. "Well, you must have pissed her off something fierce. She keeps crying and screaming obscenities about men. I won't even go into the dialog she spouted about unfaithful boyfriends."

"She caught her boyfriend cheating on her," Sean offered.

"And you are not her boyfriend?" This time, the doctor's tone was more of surprise than accusation.

For the first time in a long time, Sean was actually happy that he could answer, "No, just a friend," to this particular question before asking again about her condition.

The doctor put his hand on Sean's shoulder and guided him back to the couch before confirming what Sean had already expected. The hospital had pumped Mandi's stomach, put her on intravenous fluids and given her some adrenaline shots to help keep her conscious. The doctor felt that she would be all right but she was still in a critical period as the toxins in her blood were still at elevated stages.

"Son, this place is a madhouse tonight," the doctor continued. "We're short staffed and just don't have an extra person to sit with her all night to make sure she stays awake. However, we can check on her every two hours or so to test the toxicity of her blood to see if she is past the danger stage. Can you keep her up for a while?"

"Of course," Sean responded. Getting a good night's sleep, avoiding the flu and studying for his test all suddenly seemed unimportant.

Chapter 34

Inside Mandi's hospital room, Sean suddenly felt skittish. She looked so helpless, lying there with IV needles and tubes coming out of her, hooked up to a handful of machines.

"I feel terrible and I bet I look terrible," the young woman commented as Sean made his way to her bedside.

"You'll feel better tomorrow and you look fine," Sean retorted.

"You must think I'm an idiot," Mandi commented, avoiding eye contact.

"No," was Sean's only response.

Sean spent the next several hours with her, playing cards, trying unsuccessfully to impress the young woman with card tricks and just quietly talking.

4:30 a.m. found a nurse entering the room. As she checked the machines, she noticed how tired both students looked.

"The toxicology report shows your blood returning to safe levels. It should be all right for you to go to sleep now," the nurse said softly.

"Thanks, I'm tired," Mandi replied.

As the nurse left the room, Sean became acutely aware of how tired he had become.

"I suppose I should go," he stated as he got up to leave.

"Will you stay here on that big chair?" she requested, pointing toward a large mock-leather chair. "I'll feel better knowing that someone's here."

"Sure," he replied softly.

Her eyes were heavy and her voice little more than a whisper as she continued. Sean had to lean close to hear her.

"Why do I always seem to fall in love with the worst kind of guys?" she asked.

"Maybe you just aren't looking at the right ones."

"Yeah, but no matter how great things start out, they always seem to fall apart. They always become jerks. Is it the same with women?"

"How do you mean?"

Closing her eyes, she continued. "Well, do you find that when you start caring for a woman that she treats you like dirt? Have you ever been in love with someone who did that?"

Sean sat silently, lost in the irony of the situation. Finally, Mandi opened one eye to look at him.

"I don't think women do that," she stated abruptly, struggling to keep her eye focused on him.

"I don't think they mean to," he responded, trying to be agreeable.

"How could anyone claim to care about someone," she yawned, "and then treat them like that?"

"I don't know," he admitted as he watched her drift off to sleep.

He softly touched her hair before going over to the chair. He was elated to see the nurse return with a blanket.

"Will you please wake me at 6:10?" he requested. "I have to go to work at 6:30."

"Sure," she said, pausing briefly to look at Mandi before continuing. "She's lucky you were there looking out for her. I get the feeling she doesn't realize what she's got going for her."

Sean just nodded as the nurse turned and left.

"Good night, Mandi," he whispered as he drifted to sleep, facing toward her and hugging his blanket.

Chapter 35

Let's do this thing!"

The simple four-word phrase had been all that Nick had needed to get his head back in the game, at least temporarily. After spending another night pondering punching his coach and a senior teammate, Nick had dragged himself out of bed and gone to the morning practice.

There was never much chatter in the locker room before morning practices. Nobody seemed to have much to say at 6:15 a.m. Nick had arrived early as usual and gotten dressed without a word, still fuming about Granger and Vassec. He felt sluggish and tired, showing up more to keep up his streak of never having missed a practice than because he had a want or need to be on the mat.

Then, on his way out of the locker room, he had run into Dino. The big man looked him in the eye with an intensity that Nick rarely saw and proceeded to sock him on the shoulder, utter "Let's do this thing!" and lead him up to the wrestling room.

An hour later, Nick had gained an adrenaline high he hadn't felt in months as he and Dino pushed each other in sprints, push-ups, rope jumping, crunches and every other phase of the practice. Nobody else kept up or even seemed willing to try. This day was for Nick to match work ethics with the best in the state. JV or not, he was not going to give anyone an opening to say that he had given up.

Where the time had gone, Nick really didn't know, nor did he want to guess as the boys slowly rolled up the mats. He wanted a chance to rebuild, take his varsity spot back and get back on track toward being a champion. Moreover, he wanted it to happen now.

Practice had ended with the same intense look from Dino, accompanied by an index finger in the chest. "You keep bringing it," the big man said, "and you take it all the way to the next level."

Nick felt like he was back on the team and that he was about to become unstoppable on his journey upward.

Chapter 36

Sean was on the edge of delirium. He tried to concentrate on the test but kept losing focus. At least twice, he had drifted off to sleep, being jarred back to consciousness as his head bobbed and his body fought to stay upright.

The Physics 305 final exam subject matter wasn't that difficult. It frustrated Sean that he was struggling so with reasoning his way through his answers. He wasn't sure whether the nausea he felt was more due to disappointment in himself for not being better prepared for this exam or the flu symptoms that had taken control of his body over the past several hours, giving him the chills and churning his stomach.

Events of the past several hours were a blur. He vaguely remembered waking around 6:00, leading the morning's wrestling practice and drinking the better part of a pot of coffee as he crammed in an hour of study time before coming to the examination room. His mind drifted forward to his 'to do' list for the remainder of the day. He had hoped to stop over at the hospital and visit Mandi at some point but knew that packing for this weekend's tournament trip needed to happen sometime before the afternoon's practice.

He dreaded the upcoming trip, thinking of how it would cut into the time he had to prepare for his sister Amy's arrival. He wanted everything to be in order for their little family Christmas together. Yet what would he have to give up in order to prepare correctly? In an ideal world, he would get to spend some time with Mandi after he returned to town but before she left for the holiday break.

His gut churned. He wished that he could run out of the classroom for a moment to use the restroom but the proctor had made it clear the first time Sean had asked that leaving the exam room for any reason required him to turn in his test booklet, completed or not.

His mind drifted again to his pending trip. Road trips had been a key reason that he had joined wrestling in the first place. Even in junior high, they gave him an opportunity to get away from his father and the old man's temper.

Sean began to sweat as his eyes went blurry. "What is the answer?" he asked himself as he stared at the paper. "Answer, heck," he continued to mull, "what was the question?" He really couldn't even remember what the paper had asked. Things were snowballing to a point at which he almost didn't care.

"Please turn in your examination booklets," the proctor instructed.

Sean looked at the booklet on his desk. It was, by far, the worst work that he had ever handed in. He found consolation in the fact that it looked to be at least 90% complete. He only hoped that it would suffice to keep his A in the class and his 4.0 GPA.

Thoughts of Mandi, his wrestlers, Amy and the upcoming trip all flowed through his mind as he handed in the booklet and made a bee line for the restroom.

Chapter 37

Nick and Oscar exited the Riverside High School theater together. The student assembly they were leaving had been a bit dry but Oscar could not stop talking about the skit that the cheerleaders put on and how hot Cheri Winters had looked. Nick entered his usual state of embarrassment as Oscar went into over-zealous descriptions of the cheerleader's beauty. He changed the topic to that of the pre-Christmas tournament, coming up the next day.

Nick was particularly disappointed to be missing this tournament. It was the third largest event of the year, eclipsed only by the State tournament and January's Capital tournament. As it was held on the opposite side of the state, it was also one of the few meets at which the Riverside wrestlers stayed in a hotel. Nick hated to miss out on that potential bonding time with the team, but Oscar quickly reminded him of the objectionable events that were likely to occur.

"You know those guys are going to beat me up this weekend," the pint-sized grappler had commented.

"Of course," Nick joked. "I just wish I could be there to see it."

"I think Vassec's still irate from last week and just looking for some way to relieve his anger," Oscar continued.

Nick's mind wandered back to the prior week and Oscar getting smart with Joel on the bus. Why the kid couldn't just keep his mouth shut was a mystery to Nick. Yet he had to admit that some of the little guy's smart-aleck comments were hilarious.

As the boys reached the cafeteria, they were elated to see the cheerleaders giving out free cookies. As they got in line, Oscar resumed his commentary about how hot Cheri Winters was.

"Don't let Dino catch you talking like that," Nick warned. "Vassec is the least of your worries if you anger the big guy with your excessive comments about his would-be girlfriend."

"You're not driving up to watch the tournament?" Oscar asked, changing the subject.

"No."

"You're not quitting, are you?"

Nick had pondered this for several days now. Missing this tournament would certainly not be the end of the world for him. He was going to stay and fight. He would get his varsity position back somehow and resume his quest for the state championship, even if it meant giving up the chance to punch both Granger and Vassec.

"No!" Nick finally replied angrily, insulted that Oscar would imply that he would give up.

Having received their cookies, the boys made their way to a table and continued chatting and eating, only to be interrupted by Joel Vassec, passing by with a group of friends.

Trying to impress the female members of his group, Joel shouted to Nick and Oscar, "Those cookies are going to look real good when they are splattered all over the mat."

The older boy absorbed the giggles from his group of friends and smirked as they continued walking by.

Immediately, Oscar rose to his feet and yelled back, "So will your back!"

The entire group turned to see the little man staring Joel down and punching his right fist into his left palm.

As laughter erupted following the comment, Joel walked away angrily.

"I don't think that comment improved your chances of surviving two nights in a hotel with him this weekend," Nick noted to his friend.

"Probably not," Oscar agreed. "But burns like that only come around once in a lifetime. It was worth it."

Chapter 38

Nick felt his whole existence moving in circles. Beyond the fact that he was running laps around the wrestling room with the team, Nick felt drained. He didn't wrestle well, he was ridiculed by his teammates, he was demoralized by the school bully, he was chastised by his coach and his self esteem continued to slip, causing him to wrestle even more poorly.

The weight seemed particularly heavy this day as the varsity team prepared to leave for its trip to the pre-Christmas tournament. Nick's high from the morning's practice evaporated quickly as the time grew closer for the team to depart without him. Whether he truly belonged with them was apparently just a matter of opinion. He continued running in silence, wishing that it would all end and that he could be alone.

"Sprint," Sean yelled.

Nick and the rest of the team heeded their assistant coach's command. As tired and worn out as Nick was, he wondered why Coach MacCallister seemed to look even worse than Nick felt. The man's usual pleasant demeanor and grooming had been replaced by a zombie-like presence and large black bags under his eyes. Those same eyes were distant, lacking their usual sparkle. The stubble on his cheeks completed the unkempt picture.

Nick's attention drifted from his assistant coach to the wrestler at center mat beside the young man. This fat guy was getting a more strenuous workout than the rest of the team. Of course, it was Dino, a few pounds over weight again and working feverishly to drop them.

"Foot fire!!!" Sean yelled.

Dino ran rapidly in place.

"Sprawl!!!" Sean yelled.

Nick watched Dino as he sprawled to his belly and instantly returned to his feet, resuming foot fire status. Nick wished that he could be part of the fat group. Despite the misery that this entailed, at least Nick would be part of a group preparing to compete, and Dino wouldn't be alone.

Nick momentarily pondered how he could want to be part of a group but want to be alone at the same time. His head suddenly hurt as he contemplated that he was currently part of the wrong group and that being alone would feel better but not as good as being part of the right group. He was surprised that the sight of Coach Granger made him suddenly glad. For all of his misgivings about the man, Nick was the prisoner and Granger was the warden who was about to set him free.

"Sprawl!" Sean yelled again, sending Dino to his belly again.

"Come on, not-as-fat guys." Granger's voice followed. "Wrap it up. The bus leaves in half an hour."

The team began to disperse to the locker room with only Sean and Dino continuing their workout at center mat.

As the chatter began among the other wrestlers, Nick was more sure than ever that he didn't want to be with them in the locker room as they packed for the trip. As the rest of the team meandered toward the door, Nick first eyed and then climbed the ladder to the crow's nest.

Poking his head inside, Nick let out a sigh of relief. The crow's nest itself was a small structure protruding from the wrestling room that overlooked the school's main gym. Its main function was meant to be that of a space for television cameras to film major high school sporting events. On this night, with only volleyball practice happening in the gym, it was the perfect place for Nick to find the solitude he sought.

"Sprawl!" Sean yelled again. "Don't look away! You look at me, big man! You don't look away during a match, do you?!! You look away, I shoot, you go down, big man! That is the order of things!"

Nick crawled through the hatch and closed his eyes, wondering what the commotion was about. The one coach that Nick admired certainly knew how to light a fire and was doing so under the senior wrestler that Nick most looked up to. Nick leaned back against the wall and imagined that he was down there with them.

"Sprawl!"

The word came several more times as Nick's attention drifted to the volleyball team in the gym below him. How quickly he lost focus when there were girls within viewing distance. Somewhere along the line he lost track of time, watching the girls in their routine; serve, bump, set, spike. It was such a different sport from his. Nobody worried about cutting weight. Nick would also bet big money that getting a nose bleed due to a wicked cross-face was rare. These types of thoughts consumed his mind until he was jolted back to reality by a bump on the crow's nest door. Though startled, he was pleasantly surprised to see Dino's head appear through the hatch.

"Castle?" the older boy inquired.

"Yeah," Nick replied.

"What are you doing up here?"

Nick sat quietly for a moment pondering whether 'escaping from the team' or 'escaping from reality' would be perceived as a better answer. He finally replied with a word that was much more fitting.

"Nothing," Nick replied. Then, wanting to change the subject, he started his own line of questioning. "Are you going to make weight?"

Nick immediately realized that this was a dumb question and one that he would not want to hear in Dino's situation. He was very glad when Dino finally replied affirmatively.

Dino seemed lost in thought as he looked over the edge at the view of the gym.

"I saw you come up here. MacCallister gave me an earful for breaking eye contact," he commented. Continuing to watch the girls, he further noted, "Not a bad view though, especially with tonight's scenery."

It was nice to have company. Nick's mind drifted back to years ago when he and Ron would sit up in this spot and watch the high school wrestling matches. They would arrive for the JV matches and stay until the last varsity match ended. In between JV and varsity, they would typically retreat to the wrestling room to horse around. This usually ended with Nick getting worked over by his older brother. He didn't even realize that he was reminiscing out loud until the words left his mouth.

"Ron and I always sat up here and talked about how we were going to win all of our matches and both win state championships. It seemed so easy back then. We were going to be the first brothers to each win three consecutive state high school titles. What a joke."

"You'll make it, Nick."

Nick appreciated the older boy's support but, caught up in his own sulking, continued. "I'm not even on varsity. Why should I even bother?"

"Yeah, it's not fair is it?" Dino retorted with more than a little sarcasm. "The guys who are winning their matches get to go to the big tournament and you're left back here to feel sorry for yourself."

Nick was shocked at Dino's comment. Had he misread their friendship? What happened to the larger boy's sympathy?

"Until now," Dino continued, "I was really starting to think you had potential. But now I see what is important…you need to feel sorry for yourself. If that's the case, do it on your own time. Don't drag me into it! There is absolutely no power in your sitting here pouting. You know darn well why the coach has you sitting out. What are you going to do about it? You're not going to get your spot back sitting up here. It's time for you to take responsibility for where you're at, make a choice and move forward."

Nick suddenly got defensive and tried to interrupt but was cut off immediately.

"I know you're sick of hearing about your brother but I'll tell you why he had so much more success than you have had. The day after he lost the state championship last year, he went over to the University and practiced with their team. They threw him around quite a bit but he didn't care. He wasn't going to sit around and let 'what should have been' get in the way of being a champion. That is what we, as a team, need you to do."

"What, go practice with the University this weekend?"

"No! We need you to be a person who doesn't give up. Hermanns and Bradford smack you around daily. Still, you've never missed a practice, not even an optional one. You get here early. You leave late. You never quit. Do you think people don't notice that? All you're missing is a commitment to winning."

"I know." Nick heard the words come out of his mouth but wasn't sure exactly what he meant by them.

"Your hard work is going to pay off…but not until you decide you'll let it. Be a winner! Be the best!"

Nick looked blankly at him, not knowing whether he should be intimidated or inspired. Most of all, he didn't know what to say. He was almost happy to hear Granger's voice break the uncomfortable silence.

"Benz, quit screwing around. Get down here now!"

Dino looked sternly at Nick before quickly adding, "I've gotta go. You work out this weekend. And, don't forget what I said."

"I'm going to run with Chewie on my paper route and come in here to jump rope and lift if they'll let me. Maybe I can get some of the JV guys to come in with me," Nick responded, hoping it was the right reply.

Dino said nothing but simply held out his fist.

Nick smiled cautiously as he made a fist of his own and tapped knuckle to knuckle with Dino's fist.

Dino quickly turned and climbed down the ladder.   Nick watched his friend, pondering his own next move.

"Good luck, Benzy," the boy called out as the senior hustled out of sight.

"Be a winner. Be the best," he mumbled to himself. He then sat back to try to recall exactly what Dino's advice had been.   He remembered something about having to believe that he could win. That was bound to be a key piece of it. Nick did not realize at the time that he would spend the next several days pondering Dino's words and trying to live them.

Chapter 39

The silhouette of a wrestler stood alone in the wrestling room, quietly jumping rope. The single light in the room cast a long shadow, making the boy appear larger than he was.

Under the sweatshirt, second hooded sweatshirt and layers of tee shirts, Nick Castle's heart pounded. He couldn't think of a single other person who would be working out alone on a Saturday when everyone else in the city seemed to be on break.

Nick had to almost beg some of the other junior varsity wrestlers to come in and spar with him earlier that day. He had spent an hour practicing with the two who begrudgingly agreed to join him; one weighing 152 pounds, the other weighing 189. The larger boys had departed nearly two hours earlier, leaving Nick to himself, his workout and his thoughts.

The boy was living and breathing wrestling. He had spent the prior evening dedicated to the painful process of reviewing tapes of his matches. Ron had critiqued the tapes as they watched, a process that had taken nearly two hours as the older boy would rewind each time he saw a weakness in either Nick or his opponent and talk through ways that Nick could either improve or use opponents' shortcomings to his advantage.

For Nick, it was two hours of educational torture.

Click, click, click, the rope continued its rhythmic beat on the floor. Double time, the boy increased his intensity as his mind wandered somewhere beyond his solitude. It was a different tempo than he followed when he was running through the snow by the coulee with Chewie at the break of dawn that day. It was a different mindset altogether as he did not need to let the outside world draw his focus. He let his body go on autopilot, concentrating on his objective.

"Be the best."

Dino's words echoed in Nick's mind. How was he going to be the best when he wasn't even represented on the school's first string?

"Be the best."

The words continued their journey through his mind into his very soul.

"Be the best."

Nick wanted to follow the advice so badly. He just wished that he had some inkling of how to do so. He didn't know what to do differently. It didn't occur to him that his objective could only be obtained by pairing his actions with a complete change in his mindset.

The rope continued clicking, his heart continued pounding and Dino's voice continued echoing as the boy's workout dragged on and on.

Chapter 40

Sean felt about as lousy as he could remember as he placed the key in the lock. Now, at 3:00 a.m. on Sunday, the weekend and the tournament were already a blur. A bad blur at that.

The four-hour car trip to get to the tournament had been uneventful. Sean had downed Coke after Coke and managed to stay awake the entire way, delivering the carload of wrestlers safely to their destination halfway across the state. Wanting only to sleep and avoid the inevitable flu to whatever extent he could, Sean was horrified to find that the hotel had over-booked and the room that he had to share with Coach Granger only had one bed.

To call Granger a less-than-ideal sleeping companion would be a vast understatement. The man snored, tossed, turned and stole covers in his sleep. Sean had woken up after seven hours feeling like he had gotten less sleep than the previous night in the chair in Mandi's hospital room. The old man's comment about Sean taking the cake for being the 'ugliest woman he had ever woken up next to' hadn't made Sean feel any better.

As Sean's health had continued to decline, the team's luck seemed to follow. Joel Vassec broke his thumb in the semi-finals the first night. With the exception of Dino Benz, nobody on the team had made it to the finals. In the championship, the big man suffered his first loss of the season on a very questionable call, making the ride home a completely dismal four-hour experience for everyone involved. Nobody had talked the entire way, the wrestlers due to feeling low, Sean due to having lost his voice to the flu.

Sadly, in Sean's mind, the weekend had delivered an even worse turn than the flu, Vassec's injury, Dino's loss and Granger's sleeping habits. The young man had tried to reach Mandi on several occasions, leaving messages with the first handful of calls, then stopping at what he felt would equate to passing the 'stalker' line.

Morning, afternoon and night for two days Sean had called, needing to connect with her to make sure that she was all right. At the very least, he wanted to reach her before she left for the holiday break on Sunday morning. Not once had she picked up. He was scared stiff. Had there been complications at the hospital? Had she been released on her own and fallen back into her suicidal state with no supervision? There was no way for Sean to know, at least not until Sunday morning.

It had almost driven Sean back to drinking. He had watched Granger pound glass after glass of whisky as the man complained about the wrestlers, Joel Vassec in particular.

"The only thing worse than having my job is not having a job," Granger had grumbled.

Sean had nearly taken a swig out of Granger's bottle when the old man stumbled out to get ice. Fortunately for Sean and his sobriety trend, the head coach returned before Sean's impulse got the better of him.

Now, arriving home in the middle of the night, Sean had avoided the remnants of the fraternity's Saturday night party despite Randy's best attempts to get Sean to join the conga line he was leading. On most nights, Sean would have jumped at the chance to join in. Who could resist being part of a human chain of drunks being led by a man singing Jimmy Buffett's *One Particular Harbor* into a plastic baseball bat? On this night, it just seemed like a little much.

The key clicked in the lock and Sean pushed the door open to find Kelly engaged in his favorite pastime, watching TV on the couch.

"Wow, you look like hell," the big man commented. Sean acknowledged the comment with a nod as he dragged his duffel bag into the room and shut the door.

"How did your guys do?"

Sean wished that he could just get to bed without pushing his voice but forced out a squeaky hoarse whisper for his best friend's sake, "No champions but four guys placed in the top six in their respective weight classes. Did anyone call?"

"Please say that Mandi called," Sean thought.

"There is a message from your sister on the machine," came the reply as Kelly turned back to watching TV, not noticing Sean's disappointment.

"No calls from Mandi?" Sean clarified.

Kelly didn't even turn as he answered. "No. I saw her at the bar last night. She was half-liquored up. She looked pale."

Sean didn't know how to feel as he looked at the back of his roommate's head in disbelief. Less than 24 hours after spending a night in the hospital, the woman had gone out drinking? How could that be?

Sean felt like he needed a drink. He had felt that way all weekend as he had stared at Granger's bottle of Old Crow, but now Sean really felt like it was time for a good belt of something straight-up.

"Did you talk to her?" Sean's inquiry continued.

"No."

Sean shook his head. Could they have possibly just had that conversation? Maybe it was just the flu medicine Sean had taken? He suddenly felt very dizzy as he pulled back the covers and fell into his bunk, not even taking the time to get undressed.

There was always tomorrow. Everything would seem better tomorrow. Sean closed his eyes, said his prayers and drifted off to sleep.

Chapter 41

Sean sat in his Galaxie 500, staring at the building in front of him. It was only 10:00 a.m., surely Mandi hadn't left for the break yet. Based on Kelly's comments from their middle-of-the-night conversation, Sean would not be too surprised if the woman was still lying in bed sleeping off a hangover. He pondered whether or not it was odd for him to be showing up uninvited. Since he had failed at all other attempts to reach her to say 'goodbye', he decided that it wasn't an issue.

The wind was brisk as Sean walked to the building door. He worried a bit that it would mess up his hair. On this particular morning, Sean had spent extra time on his appearance, doing his best to cover up the fact that he was still under the weather. He was weak and achy but that wouldn't be apparent externally. His eyes may give this fact away but he made certain that his hair, breath and cleanly shaven face did not. He had even slipped on his best sweater to draw attention from whichever of his features was crying out, "I'm ill, stay away!"

Sean stopped momentarily to check his hair in the glass of the fire extinguisher box. His thoughts were on his voice as he continued on to Mandi's door. He knew he couldn't disguise that little issue but also realized that it had probably already come across in the voice messages he had left.

Unlike his last experience in this hallway, Sean did not wait to knock. Four quick raps followed by another three. He was relieved and happy to hear Mandi's voice immediately respond, "Just a minute."

He stood there for a moment, listening to the scurrying noises coming from the other side of the door and pondering exactly what he was going to say. His mind raced from subject to subject. He would tell her that she looked great, no matter how she looked. He would also ask her how the day after their night at the hospital had gone for her. He would ask her about her pending trip home and try to somehow work in the question about whether or not she had gotten his messages. It really didn't matter at this point. He was mainly happy that he would get to see her prior to her departure.

The door opened and Mandi stood there in her pajamas with a major case of 'bed hair'. To most people, she probably would have looked repulsive but to Sean, she looked irresistible. It wouldn't be a lie when he got around to telling her how nice she looked. She certainly seemed surprised to see him.

"Hey Mac…" she started in a hesitant voice.

Sean smiled for a moment as he opened his mouth to speak. Unexpectedly, he was cut off by a man's voice from inside the apartment.

"Who is it?" the voice asked.

Sean tensed up, suddenly feeling very awkward and confused. Mandi's face showed that she felt the same as she quickly inserted, "Now isn't a good time," as if the sentiment hadn't been clear the moment Sean had heard the man's voice.

Sean stood for a second, not having any idea what he should say, feel or think. He momentarily pondered whose voice could be coming from the other room before the horrifying reality hit him. Sean's worst nightmares were realized as Ted Graham came around the corner, wearing a sweatshirt and sweat pants. His hair was as disheveled as Mandi's.

As Sean's shock quickly turned to anger, he glared at the man and quickly turned and walked away. He knew that if he stayed any longer, he would boil over and pummel Ted. It wasn't something that he wanted or needed on his record.

"Mac," Mandi called after him as he made his way down the hall.

Sean was too furious to even look back at her. His only response to her voice was to hold his hand up in a half-hearted wave and mutter "You're so freaking stupid," both to her and himself under his breath.

She continued to speak but he tuned out everything except his own jumbled thoughts as he turned from the main hallway to exit the building as quickly as he could.

Chapter 42

Sean stared at the wall, his mind filling with fog. He wondered how his life could possibly get any worse. The events of the last several days had made him completely numb. He had returned from Mandi's apartment more than twelve hours earlier to find that Kelly had already left for Christmas.

In Sean's experience, the best way to rebound from feeling down was to spend time with friends. Unfortunately, on this particular day, he had crawled back into bed, fully clothed and alternated between sleeping and listening as door after door shut and latched as each of his fraternity brothers went home for the holidays.

Home. The word held a different meaning to Sean than it did to the others. When Sean talked about going home, he meant the exact spot where he currently lay. He didn't leave this place to visit his parents. The house he had grown up in was a place that only passed through his mind as a nightmare. His home was here, with his brothers. 'Home for the holidays' was supposed to be in this very house, with his sister Amy visiting him. That plan had all changed when he listened to her message.

"Hi big brother, it's me," the message began. "I'm not going to make it to your place. I just spent $250 getting my car worked on and it still doesn't want to start right. My suite mate, Sandy, said I can go home with her and I think I'm going to take her up on it. Call me if you get the chance, we're not leaving until late. Love you big brother."

The message had been left two days before Sean had received it. The fact that he hadn't even been able to catch her 'voice to voice' only made matters worse. The only thing that he really had to look forward to at this point was the daily wrestling practice.

By mid-afternoon, everyone else had left. Sean had spent the remainder of the day watching TV and reading. At 11:00 p.m., he rightly wondered how he would keep from going stir crazy, alone in this confined space. Twelve hours of solitude had been bad enough. How would he make it through two weeks?

It was unfortunate timing for Sean to notice the note on Kelly's refrigerator. *Merry Christmas*, it read, *I left you a present in the fridge in case you need some Christmas cheer. It should be just the right temperature for sipping. Kelly*

Sean opened the door to find a bottle of rum with a bow on it.

He paced around for the next hour, killing time by working on a plan for the next day's wrestling practice, paging through some of his text books and generally wandering aimlessly around the house and his room. As his clock flipped to midnight, Sean wrote "167" on Sunday, December 21st, then immediately opened the refrigerator and pulled out the rum bottle.

He had lost all confidence, self control and desire to stay sober. He had slept too much during the day to have any chance of falling asleep on his own any time soon. He reasoned that, if he didn't take a drink tonight, he certainly would sometime over the next couple of days. With the team breaking on the 25th for Christmas, he wouldn't even have wrestling practice to keep him occupied. It would surely be a day for him to fall off the wagon. Doing so a few days in advance would be far less sacrilegious.

Sean examined the bottle closely as he set it on his desk. He cracked the seal, removed the cap and inhaled deeply, letting the fumes penetrate his olfactory sensors. The liquid smelled wonderful. The young man got hazy just from the fumes and suddenly felt guilty. He had gone nearly half a year without a drink and now he was about to tie one on all by himself. Sean prayed for forgiveness rather than strength as he found a glass, set it next to the bottle and paused to ponder what he was about to do.

A knock on the door caused Sean to jump from his chair and nearly soil himself. He knew for certain that everyone else living in the house had departed for the holiday break. Who could possibly be knocking on his door in the middle of the night? It could be a prowler, he reasoned, but would a prowler knock?

"Hello?" Sean finally managed to ask.

Sean braced himself as the door opened and was relieved as Otis, the quiet pledge, entered his doorway.

"Hey Sean," the younger man said.

From Otis's clothing, it was clear that he had just gotten off of work at the McDonald's up the street. It hadn't occurred to Sean that any of the pledges would be staying in town. Why the young man was here didn't matter. All that mattered at this point was that Sean wasn't alone. He recapped the bottle, invited the younger man inside and thanked God for sending Otis into his life.

"Are you doing anything for Christmas?" Otis asked. "Are you going to see your family?"

Sean stared half-bleary-eyed at the young man. If Otis only knew about Sean's family and how much he wished that he could have a normal Christmas, the question never would have been asked. Still, Otis didn't know. How could he?

"No, I'm just staying here and working," Sean finally replied. "How about you?"

"My mom and dad are coming here and staying at the Ramada Inn," the younger man replied. "If you want to come over and spend some time with us, I know that they would love to meet you. They know you're the reason that I'm still here."

Sean was taken aback by the comment. Had Otis really been planning to leave school? The thought made Sean pause briefly before replying.

"Yeah, I'd like that," he finally uttered.

Sean was amazed that, once again, his fraternity family had come through for him in ways that his biological family never had. He wondered if he looked as grateful as he felt as he accepted the invitation for a true family Christmas.

Chapter 43

Nick paced in the hall for another couple of seconds and then marched into the coaches' office. He had made up his mind that he would confront Granger and ask for a shot at getting his varsity spot back.

Based on the way the coach removed him from varsity in the first place, the thought of a potential confrontation scared the daylights out of Nick. The only new ammunition he had was the fact that Mack had been pinned in both of his matches at the pre-Christmas tournament. It would be hard for Granger to argue that Nick could do worse than that, although Nick wouldn't put it past the man.

Nick nearly bumped into Colin Bradford on his way into the office as the senior walked out. Nick breathed an extra sigh of relief as he saw Coach MacCallister seated opposite Coach Granger. For whatever reason, Nick felt more comfortable around the younger coach. It was almost as if the man was Nick's advocate.

"Coach?" Nick asked, not exactly knowing how to pursue the subject.

Both coaches turned to face the boy. Nick noted that Granger's face held its usual aggravated expression. Yet, he had left himself without a way to turn back, so he continued.

"I'd like a wrestle-off with Mack to get my spot back."

Granger looked at Sean who simply nodded his head. Nick got a quick gleam of hope from the exchange.

"How much do you weigh?" the head coach asked.

Nick's heart suddenly fell into his shoes. His weight would be a major piece of artillery in Granger's arsenal. Yet, he couldn't lie as he knew that Granger would put him on a scale sometime that day.

"143 pounds," Nick began. Then, seeing Granger's frustrated look, he quickly added, "but I can make it down to 137 by Saturday. It's no problem at all."

The first tournament of the new year was only three days away. Nick was going to use the fact that all wrestlers were given two 'growth pounds' at the turn of the year to his advantage. He didn't know who had made the initial argument that it wasn't healthy for teenage boys to keep cutting to the same weight the entire season without regard to the fact that their bodies were growing, but he was very happy with the ruling which allotted him two extra pounds for the second half of the season.

Granger's reply was short and to the point, "You'd have to weigh in at 135."

Nick started to get frustrated again. Didn't the man know about the two pounds?

"But we get two pounds after the new year," the boy began to argue as he watched his head coach roll his eyes.

"In high school, that works slightly different than junior high," Granger started with an irritated expression. "At the last tournament before Christmas, which you happened to miss, wrestlers have to get certified at scratch weight. Those wrestlers, who are certified, get an extra two pounds after the turn of the year. Because you weren't there, you will have to get certified at 135 before you get the extra two pounds. I don't want you to cut eight pounds in three days. You'll have to wait until the next dual to wrestle off."

Nick's head was spinning. He couldn't believe that he didn't know this rule and his hope was quickly diminishing. If he didn't wrestle at this tournament, he would have to wait another few weeks to prove himself. What would be the coach's excuse that time? Nick felt as if the entire season was disappearing before his eyes.

"What about 140?"

Nick turned to see where the question had originated. Coach MacCallister sat looking to Coach Granger for a response.

"With Bradford at his sister's wedding, we have a vacancy at 140," the young man continued. "Why don't we give the spot to Nick?"

"I'm not going to feed him to those wolves," was Granger's only rebuttal.

"He's above their weight right now. Besides, we don't lose anything by putting him on the mat," Sean continued before looking to Nick and asking, "Are you up for moving to 140?"

Nick couldn't think of a reason to not accept.

"I'll do it," he replied.

"He can weigh in at 140," Granger agreed reluctantly. "But, if he gets bulled around his first match, I'm pulling him out."

"Agreed," Nick responded.

The boy felt high as a kite. He hadn't gotten his own varsity spot back but this one would do for now. It was all just a matter of taking things one step at a time. He didn't know exactly why, but he felt that this round had gone to him.

Chapter 44

Nick felt a little guilty as he crunched on his apple. He knew that others on the bus, including Dino who was sitting directly in front of him, were struggling to make weight. Yet, for the first time this season, Nick was leaving for a tournament weighing a pound less than he needed to. He felt like he owed it to himself to eat something to keep his strength up.

His mind wandered back to getting ready that morning. He had hoped that Ron would make the trip to see his reappearance on varsity but his brother had made it very clear that he wasn't going to any more wrestling tournaments, and that this tournament in particular was a sore spot as Ron had prevailed as champion the prior year. The last thing the older boy wanted was to see his name in the paper again in some sympathy story about a former champion being sidelined.

Nick understood his brother's frustration but still wanted him there. He wished that there were a way to keep his brother incognito so that they could watch matches together while Nick waited to wrestle. He would welcome any such feeling like their old days in junior high. Nick regularly won matches back then. He pondered what could possibly be missing that kept him from winning now. Could it possibly be that lack of familiarity that came from his brother not being there? Whatever the missing piece was, Nick felt that he needed some kind of boost to get him back into that rhythm. The key was to figure out what would give him that boost.

Nick looked ahead a few rows to where Joel Vassec sat. The boost certainly wasn't coming from that crowd. Even this morning, the older boy had taken the time to ridicule him about the possibility of not making weight. Nick pulled the apple away from his mouth as he thought about the embarrassment he would face if he didn't make weight in the weight class above his regular one. He eyed the fruit suspiciously as he held it in his hand. Surely it couldn't weigh a pound.

"I'll make it," he whispered in Joel's direction as he finished the snack.

Chapter 45

Sean left the seeding meeting and walked quickly down the hall. Events in the meeting had gone awry, leaving Sean with only a few minutes to ensure that his plan to boost Nick's confidence didn't get shattered in the first round.

In Sean's mind, the small tournament's nine-team format created the perfect opportunity to get Nick back on the winning track. The boy's dismal record would surely require that he wrestle someone having an equally lackluster season in a wrestle-in round. Sean felt confident that Nick could win, setting up a match against the top seed in the next round. Winning was unlikely against the top seed, who was currently ranked third in the state, but if Nick wrestled competitively, he would likely have the confidence to do well in subsequent rounds against less talented athletes.

Unfortunately, all of Sean's hopes had been shattered as one coach announced that he didn't have a wrestler at 140 pounds. This eliminated the need for the wrestle-in round and pitted Nick against the top seed in his first match. Sean feared that, if the boy got pummeled, Granger would pull him from the tournament completely, further eroding Nick's dwindling self-esteem.

Yet, there was a bright spot in all of this. Sean remembered the top seed, Jason Oaks. He had seen him wrestle at the pre-Christmas tournament. As well as he had wrestled, placing second, Sean knew of a weak spot that made him vulnerable.

Sean's memory went back to the tournament. Sitting with Dino, the two had joked about how Oaks' uniform was cut wrong. On two occasions, Oaks had taken a shot and missed. In each of those two instances, he had gotten back to his feet, stood straight up and pulled on the bottom of his singlet to remove a wedgie from his rear. This left the boy's legs exposed, creating an opportunity for a well-prepared wrestler to take a shot and take him down.

The big challenge at this point would be in ensuring that Nick was aware of his opponent's weakness while simultaneously keeping the boy's impressive twelve and two record a secret.

Granger had taken a vow of silence. Sean would need to ensure that the team did the same.

Sean walked briskly down the hall, eager to communicate his message.

Chapter 46

Nick sat alone, quietly tying his shoes. He was so focused on winning his first match that he didn't even notice the figure enter the locker room and choose a locker just across the aisle from where Nick was sitting.

Nick would shoot today. He had been wrestling far too defensively recently. In practices the past few days, he had gotten good penetration on Bradford, even taking the older boy down on several occasions. Nick would be aggressive and it would be the key to getting back on the winning track.

"Are you little Castle?"

The voice startled Nick and pulled his thoughts away from the future. He looked over to see Travis Spegidos donning his uniform and gear.

"Yeah," Nick replied cautiously. "You're Spegidos, right?"

There was really no need for the question. Nick knew exactly who the boy was. For that matter, every wrestler in the state knew who the boy was. He was a junior, currently the top 130-pound wrestler in the state. He was thought by many to be one of the best wrestlers the state had ever seen. A state champion as a freshman, the boy had gone undefeated his sophomore year until he had reached the state tournament's semi-finals. There, he had lost in overtime to none other than Ron Castle, helping to solidify the legend of Nick's older brother.

Spegidos nodded an affirmation before continuing with another question.

"Why are you wearing number seven? I thought you were wrestling 135."

Nick thought nothing of rambling on about Bradford's sister's wedding. He was starting to feel cautiously comfortable with the older boy until he noticed Spegidos was putting on uniform number six.

Nick's blood froze. Spegidos should be wearing uniform number five like everyone else in the 130-pound weight class. Why was he wrestling up a weight? Surely he hadn't lost his varsity spot. Nick remembered back to last year's state tournament and the fit this boy had thrown when Ron won their match. He had been blood-thirsty, out for revenge. Nick suddenly felt like he was the prey in some big game hunt. For the first time, he was relieved to have moved up to 140.

"Why are you wrestling 135?" Nick asked cautiously.

Spegidos was shorter than Nick, probably only five foot seven. What he lacked in height, he made up for in muscle. His physique was impeccable. His large arms, shoulders and chest looked like they were carved in granite.

"You weren't at the pre-Christmas tournament."

Nick was further unnerved by the boy's choice to ignore his question. It made him all the more suspicious.

"No," Nick replied.

"How come?"

"I missed making weight once and lost my spot."

"Is your brother going to make a full recovery?"

Nick was getting more and more uneasy with every passing second and each question.

"He's a lot better now. He has another surgery this week," Nick answered as he gathered his things to leave.

"Is he going to wrestle again? He was pretty good."

Nick felt his heart race as he started making his way toward the door, further unnerved to see that Spegidos had decided to accompany him.

"He can't walk," Nick eventually replied. He felt Spegidos' cold stare upon him and suddenly didn't want to have anything to do with the boy. Nick was elated to see the locker room door open and Coach MacCallister walk in. He was a bit confused as to why the man was wearing gym shorts, wrestling shoes and a tee shirt.

"Bye," Nick said to Spegidos as he walked toward the exit.

The older boy's lack of response made it clear to Nick that he was only being used for information in what seemed like a dangerous game.

Chapter 47

It's time to warm up, you're coming with me," Sean commanded.

Nick followed like a puppy, joining the man in his trip to the wrestling room.

Practice mats were laid out and a few wrestlers were taking advantage of the facility, either stretching or warming up.

"Have you been watching for 140-pounders?" Sean asked, trying to gain a feel for Nick's familiarity with his opponents.

"I saw a couple at weigh in," Nick replied. "I didn't really recognize anyone. I mainly know the 135 guys."

Sean smiled as he realized that his plan was actually sprouting legs.

"Well, we got you someone in the first round that you should match up well against. You know how the wrestle-in round works, right? The guys with the lowest winning percentages wrestle against each other for the opportunity to face the top seed."

Sean was careful to not lie. At this point, he only needed to speak vaguely and bend the truth.

"Yeah," Nick replied.

"Well, this kid is two and twelve," Sean continued. This was borderline true as Sean had swapped the wins and losses but, in his mind, since he hadn't specifically stated that the boy had won only two matches, he could eventually explain that away as well.

"Really?"

"Yeah, I saw him wrestle at the pre-Christmas tournament. He looks tough and confident but he has a major weakness that you can exploit. Do you want to know how to beat him?"

"Of course," Nick replied eagerly. He was ready for any and all information that would get him back on the winning track.

Sean got into his stance, facing Nick as if the two were going to wrestle.

"He's a shooter," Sean started. "You need to know right away that he's going to think he can shoot on you."

Sean shot a shallow single leg shot, against which Nick sprawled and quickly returned to his feet.

"Good, Nick. Now, when you sprawl and both come back to your feet, he's going to stand straight up and pull his singlet out of his butt crack. What are you going to do?"

Nick started laughing at the thought of this scene. He couldn't help himself.

"Offer him some toilet paper?" the boy replied with a smile.

"Don't be smart. Do you want to win or not?"

"Shoot on him!" Nick countered, happy that this true answer matched well with his original game plan.

"Bingo," Sean answered with a smile.   "Now let's work on that."

As the two sparred, Sean could feel Nick's confidence grow each time Nick took a shot. He only hoped that it would be enough against a superior wrestler.

Chapter 48

Nick looked into Coach MacCallister's eyes.

"Go get him!" the man said.

The wrestler's body filled with adrenaline. It was the most excited that Nick had been for a match all year. He was going to bring everything he had and felt the win imminent in his system. He marched to the center of the mat and put the green leg band around his ankle.

Nick eyed his opponent. The boy certainly appeared arrogant for someone of his record. Then again, perhaps he had seen Nick's record and felt that this was a good chance to get a scarce win.

The two faced each other and began feeling each other out. Oaks tried to push Nick around. Nick tried for an arm drag that didn't go anywhere. Finally, Oaks shot in with surprising quickness on a double leg shot that sent both wrestlers out of bounds.

"Sprawl when he does that!" Coach Granger yelled.

Nick nodded as he returned to the center of the mat. He had to admit this time that his head coach was right. Perhaps Nick had taken too much credit away from his opponent. He locked in his mind that he needed to give the boy some kind of credit or become a victim of overconfidence and end up with another loss.

As the two wrestlers again faced each other at the center of the mat, the ref blew his whistle. Immediately, Oaks shot at Nick's legs. Nick sprawled, pushed away and got right back to his feet. Events seemed to move in slow motion as Oaks also returned to his feet, stood straight up and pulled on the bottom of his singlet.

Nick's own words of "Shoot on him" echoed in the boy's mind as he took a double leg shot, catching his opponent off guard and driving the boy to the mat.

The referee's call of "Two points green" echoed somewhere in the back of Nick's mind along with what he thought may have been some cheering. None of it mattered. As Oaks fought to get to his belly and then to his hands and knees, Nick put in both legs and pounded his opponent's forearms with his own fists, causing the boy to do a face plant into the mat.

Nick wrestled the entire match in a similar fashion, looking like a boy possessed and battling toe to toe with the older boy. It all seemed to pass too quickly as Nick found himself in the third period, down by a score of eight to ten.

Nick was feeling a bit winded, but not as much so as Oaks. The older boy seemed to be having trouble catching his breath. From his position on the bottom, Nick could hear his opponent gasping for air. Nick burst forward, struggled to his feet and turned to face Oaks who immediately grabbed Nick and threw him back to the mat.

"One point green, two points red," yelled the ref. The comment was immediately met by a tirade from Nick's corner.

"What?!! He never lost control!" Granger yelled.

Nick began getting frantic as he saw the girl with the towel begin walking toward them. He let his hyperventilating opponent secure one leg between his own and immediately hooked it, rolled through and ended up on top and in control, securing the reversal.

"Two points green," the referee called.

Nick worked desperately to turn Oaks but waning time and a one-point lead were his opponent's allies. The girl with the towel tapped the referee on the back, causing him to blow the whistle, ending the match.

Nick was nearly in tears he was so mad. How could he have let this one slip away? He shook his opponent's hand and watched in pain as the referee raised the other boy's arm. Granger's voice was immediately barking in his ear. Yet, this time, the man wasn't yelling at Nick, he was yelling at the referee.

"He did not lose control on that supposed escape!" the coach growled, getting in the referee's face.

"Do NOT tell me how to referee the match!" the man in stripes retorted.

"Someone needs to!" Granger replied as he stomped back to Nick's corner. "You were robbed," he told Nick. "You would have smoked that kid in overtime. Look at him, he can barely stand."

Somehow, neither his head coach's sudden confidence in him nor his ailing opponent made the loss any easier. Nick was down on himself and ready to quit, having found yet another way to snatch a defeat from the jaws of victory.

"I had him," Nick complained, throwing in a few curse words of frustration.

"Watch the language, Nick, there are parents here," Coach MacCallister sternly advised.

"But I had him, he sucks," Nick repeated, adding extra curses and pulling on his warm-up shirt before starting to walk away.

The grasp on his arm felt like steel and stopped the boy in his tracks. Nick wheeled around with his fist cocked, ready to hit whoever it was. Seeing Coach MacCallister's face, Nick felt relieved as this was one of the only people in the world he was not willing to strike at this point.

The assistant coach led him to a quiet spot near the bleachers and handed him the tournament program.

"Open it to 140," the young man instructed.

Nick begrudgingly followed orders, reluctant to see what his coach wanted to show him. He was surprised and a little confused as his eyes fell on the 140-pound bracket where his name was not listed in a wrestle-in but rather slotted in against the number one seed.

"He's not so bad, Nick. That kid that you just took to his limits and nearly beat is ranked third in the state. He took second at the big pre-Christmas tournament and has only lost two matches this season."

"But you told me..." Nick started.

"I told you he was two and twelve. You never asked which number was 'wins' and I intentionally didn't offer it. I knew that you could wrestle up to his level if you believed you were equals and you proved me right. It's all up here, Nick," Coach MacCallister instructed, putting an index finger on Nick's temple. "You just proved that you can wrestle with anyone in this state, or any other state for that matter. It just took a little minor deception to prove it to you. I had confidence in you, even if you didn't."

Nick just stared blankly at the man. He didn't know whether he should reconsider his decision to not punch him in the chops or to give him a hug. In the end, he opted for neither. He believed that he had just cleared the hurdle he had been bemoaning that morning.

"You did alright, kid," Coach MacCallister said, patting the bewildered youth on the back. "You did alright."

Chapter 49

Nick felt on top of the world as he stood on the platform. He looked at the three boys who had placed above him and wondered what would have happened if he had been given the chance to face the runner-up. Jason Oaks had won every match with relative ease with the exception of his match against Nick. In the championship match, he had won by virtue of a technical fall, beating his opponent by fifteen points before the match was stopped in the second period.

"You wrestled a heck of a tournament today, Castle," the champion had told him as the two walked to their respective steps. "Next time, I won't underestimate you."

"Next time," Nick thought, "I'll win."

For the first time ever, Coach Granger had spoken highly of Nick, marveling at the way the boy had completely out-lasted a senior in overtime, enabling him to win by two points and make it into the consolation championship. Even though he ended up losing his final match, it again had been a fight to the finish with Nick coming on late, outscoring his opponent by five points in the final period but still falling two points shy of winning.

Perhaps Dino had been Nick's greatest supporter, bragging about the boy's accomplishments in the locker room after winning his own title.

"You moved up a weight class and went toe to toe with some of the highest ranked guys in the state," the senior had commended the boy. "You just showed everyone that there is a new Castle to beware of."

Nick smiled as he reveled in the moment. It was a day in which it seemed that everyone was on his side.

"You have a lot to be proud of," Coach MacCallister had offered.

For some reason, Nick believed that to be true.

Chapter 50

Nick felt odd. He had spent so many hours in the wrestling room that it felt like a second home to him. It was just that, on this particular day at this particular time, he felt the walls closing in, like he was in some foreign land, surrounded by strangers.

The reason for his discomfort was fairly simple. Rather than being surrounded by his teammates, this day was the lone session of wrestling conducted for Nick's Gym class. He looked around to see boys of all shapes, sizes and attitudes. Mostly, he looked across the mat at Todd Johnson and his cronies. Even in this, Nick's safe zone, the bully and his pals still intimidated Nick. The group joked around and looked at Nick as the Gym teacher, Mr. McNeely, gave instructions. Nick sat quietly, knowing that one member of the group, Tim Parks, was closest to Nick's weight and would be his partner for today's drills.

"Now that you know some technique, we're going to wrestle a match. I think even those of you who are in shape will find that it wears you down quickly. We'll go for three minutes," Mr. McNeely explained. "Take your partners."

As Nick got to his feet, the tensions started to subside. As well as he had done in the prior weekend's tournament against some of the state's best, Tim shouldn't be much of a challenge. He let a wry smile cross his lips.

"What's so funny, Cass-hole?" the boy questioned. "In a couple of seconds, you're not going to have a face to smile with."

Nick silently assumed his neutral stance. His focus was changing from that of student to that of wrestler.

The Gym teacher blew his whistle and Tim immediately moved in for the attack, trying to tie up Nick's arms. Nick avoided his aggression by popping both of Tim's arms upward, ducking down and shooting a double leg takedown. As part of the maneuver, he briefly lifted Tim into the air before driving the boy hard to the mat, knocking the wind out of him. It was a partial payback for the day fall semester when Tim had found it necessary to kick Nick's books down the hall.

As Nick pondered his next move, he allowed Tim to turn on his belly. Almost instinctively, Nick slammed his upper arm into Tim's cheekbone, grabbing the boy's far arm in the process. He then cupped the boy's far leg, drove Tim's head toward his leg and locked his own hands, cradling Tim before putting him to his back.

The two lay there for a moment before Nick realized that there was no referee to count the pin. There was a sharp pain in Nick's fingers as Tim began digging his fingernails into Nick's knuckles, trying to peel off skin. Nick let go and pushed the boy away.

Tim began laughing as he got to his feet, leaving his legs completely exposed. Nick shot a second double leg takedown and again put Tim into the mat hard, knocking the wind out of him as the teacher blew the whistle to end the first period.

The next two periods were very much the same as Nick used his technique and agility to continue his attack until the teacher finally blew the whistle, ending Tim's misery.

"I'm going to kill you!" Tim commented as the two separated for the final time.

Nick could only smile as he replied, "Whatever," and joined the rest of the class in a circle around the teacher.

"Nick, I saw you shooting some double legs," Mr. McNeely commented. "Do you want to demonstrate for the class in slow motion?"

Nick suddenly felt sick again, wishing that he had not shown off his repertoire against Tim. Now he would have to be the center of attention, the situation which made him completely uneasy. He looked around nervously as he reluctantly accepted and approached the teacher.

"Thanks Nick," the teacher remarked. "I'll be the practice dummy. I'm not that heavy."

Turning his attention back to the class, the teacher explained, "You will see as Nick shoots…"

Nick shot in and grabbed Mr. McNeely's legs.

"…stop right there."

Nick stopped below the Gym teacher with his right leg between the teacher's legs, his right foot firmly planted on the mat, his left knee on the mat and both of his arms around the teacher's legs.

Not wanting to miss an opportunity, Todd Johnson commented, "That looks like a natural position for you, Castle," causing his cronies and others in the class to snicker.

The teacher ignored Todd and continued, "You will see that his foot is planted." He pointed to Nick's right foot before instructing the boy, "Continue."

Nick rolled forward, using his legs to pick the teacher off the mat, leaving the man at his mercy, stranded in the air.

"From here, it's pretty much up to him to decide how to finish it."

Nick gently finished the move by putting the teacher softly to his back on the mat.

"Technique is important," the teacher continued as he got back to his feet. "A wrestler with good technique will often beat a stronger opponent whose technique is less polished. Right, Nick?"

Shyly, Nick agreed, not knowing if this was a compliment directed toward him or, hopefully just a general rule of thumb.

Not wanting Nick to end on a high note, Todd Johnson chimed in, sarcastically commenting, "How would you know what a good wrestler can do, Castle?"

The Gym teacher looked as if he had almost expected such ribbing from Todd. Perhaps he remembered the incident at the pre-Christmas dance? He took advantage of the opportunity. "Mr. Johnson, you seem to know what you're doing. Would you care to come out and show your technique against Mr. Castle?"

Nick's blood ran cold. Not only was there potential to be the center of attention, he would have to do so facing the one person who had made his life the most miserable this year. He secretly hoped that Todd would decline. What if Nick lost? He would never hear the end of it, even though Todd outweighed him by at least seventy pounds. "Please say, 'no'," the boy thought as his heart began to race.

To Nick's dismay, Todd got to his feet and walked to the center of the mat, a huge smirk crossing his face. "I'm glad I get to shower after this," the boy commented to his audience. "It makes me a little bit sick that I have to touch this guy, even if it is just to smack him around."

Nick didn't bother replying. There wasn't anything to say. He got up and began focusing on the task at hand. How could he take down someone he couldn't lift? How could he gain control over someone who only had to fall on him to flatten him? For some reason, Nick began to relax as he gained faith that the answers would appear on their own.

One by one, Nick's other classmates disappeared from his world as the boy approached the center of the mat, until the only beings that seemed to exist were Nick and Todd. By the time he reached his opponent, it was no longer Todd but some nameless, faceless, overweight, clumsy lump of flesh.

The Gym teacher's words, "Show us what you've learned, boys. A three-minute match." echoed somewhere in the background as Nick shook Todd's hand.

"Wrestle!"

Nick froze as Todd pushed forward into him like a bulldozer, driving him off the mat.

"Stop and come back to the center," the Gym teacher instructed.

Todd pushed Nick's shoulder as the two walked back. Nick was too deep in thought for the cheap shot to register.

"Wrestle!"

Todd again pushed Nick, driving into the boy with all of his weight. As he did so, Nick grabbed the back of the bigger boy's neck, ducked under his opposite arm and used his opponent's own weight and momentum to take him down, straight to his belly.

"Two points, Castle," the teacher announced.

Surprised and angry, Todd began to get up. As he got to his hands and knees, Nick aligned himself on the bigger boy's back, sitting on Todd's lower back and putting both of his legs between Todd's legs, locking the boy up.

A voice appeared in Nick's mind, much clearer than that of anyone who was in the room. He heard Dino's comment from the month before, "I like to put in both legs and crank on guys like that sometimes and not let them turn. It's just a reminder that they're not as indestructible as they think they are."

Nick immediately slammed his left forearm into the back of Todd's neck. Getting his right arm beneath Todd's, he locked his hands and began wrenching on the half nelson like there was no tomorrow.

"Twenty seconds left in the period," he heard the teacher say.

It didn't matter how much time was left. As Todd tried time and time again to get back up to a solid base, Nick continued kicking the boy's legs out from under him and wrenching on his opponent's neck and shoulder with every ounce of strength he could muster.

"That's the end of the first period. Castle two, Johnson zero."

As Nick let go of his hold, Todd pushed him. The bigger boy was clearly embarrassed and angry, not to mention physically aching from Nick's assault.

"Mr. Johnson, as you are behind, I'll give you the choice. You can be up, down, neutral, or defer and let Mr. Castle choose," Mr. McNeely instructed.

Immediately, Todd chose 'up', wanting an opportunity to give Nick a taste of his own medicine. He was smiling as he saw Nick get to his hands and knees in the center of the mat.

It took Mr. McNeely a moment to show Todd the proper form for mounting. As the teacher walked away and re-set his stopwatch, Todd whispered to Nick, "You're dead, Cass-hole."

"Ready...wrestle."

It took a millisecond for Nick to burst forward, plant a foot and rise to one knee. In the same motion, he threw his right elbow back and felt the dull thud as it made contact with his opponent. As he continued to scramble forward, he felt Todd let go. Nick scrambled to his feet securing an escape. His mind raced as he considered his situation. He would need to press his attack quickly before Todd got his bearings.

As Nick turned to face his opponent, he was met with a scene he didn't expect. Todd was on his knees, holding his nose with both hands. Blood was clearly visible, dripping from the bottoms of both of Todd's hands.

"Hit him again, Castle!!!" one of the other students yelled.

The entire picture brought Nick back to reality. He had been lost for a few minutes, focusing only on saving face and beating this opponent. Now, whatever his goal had been was forgotten. He looked down on his injured classmate and could not help but feel sorry for the boy.

"Stop!" the Gym teacher yelled. "Todd, lie down on your back and keep holding that nose. The rest of you guys, go shower up."

As the teacher went to tend to Todd, Nick walked with the other boys toward the locker room. However, instead of joining them as they walked down the stairs, he opened the med-kit, just inside the room and dug some cotton out for Todd.

"You're dead, Castle," Tim Parks threatened as he passed behind Nick. Nick immediately reeled and cocked his fist at the boy, catching Tim off guard and nearly causing him to trip and fall down the stairs.

It was a new day for Nick Castle. He no longer had any fear of Todd Johnson and he certainly wasn't going to take any grief from the boy's lesser cronies. If they wanted to try to pick on him, that was fine but there was no way that he would let any of them intimidate him.

Nick approached Todd with the cotton and met the boy's glare without blinking. The Gym teacher was finishing toweling up Todd's blood and noticed the non-verbal exchange.

"The match is over, shake hands," the man commanded.

Nick reluctantly extended his hand. To his surprise, Todd did the same and the two boys shook.

"I'm sorry about your nose," Nick apologized, handing a wad of cotton to Todd. "If you stuff some of this up there and lie with your head back, it will clot up in a couple of minutes."

He knelt silently for another half minute as Todd pushed the cotton into his nostrils. He then nodded at the boy and left for the locker room.

Chapter 51

Ron shot on Spegidos, picked the boy off the mat and put him straight to his back. Immediately, the ref blew his whistle, signaling that Ron had won and raised the boy's hand.

Tony Simms stepped onto the mat before Ron could leave. Ron felt prepared, shook the wrestler's hand and immediately shot in with a fireman's carry. With a single fluid motion, he took Simms from his feet to his back and held him there until he heard the referee slap the mat. Again, Ron stood triumphant as the referee held his hand in the air.

Ron felt alive, he felt free as the crowd charged the mat, picking him up and placing him on their shoulders. It was a feeling so positive and familiar to the wrestler. He felt like he was on top of the world as they carried him around and took his picture.

Suddenly, they set him down, to his horror, in a wheel chair. He tried to get out but his legs wouldn't move. The cameras flashed as he tried to wheel himself away to no avail. He was completely fenced in by the mob of people.

Members of the media yelled to him, trying to get his attention.

"Ron!" said a man in a brown suit.

Ron turned away, trying to wheel himself in the opposite direction but ran headlong into two other reporters. He began to sweat and panic as they tried to put their microphones in his face.

"Ron! Ron?" they said as he tried to evade their cameras and questions.

He didn't want to be there. He didn't want anyone to see him like this. He just wanted to get away.

Ron sat straight up in his bed, sweating as if it were a hundred degrees in his room and startling his younger brother who was standing over him.

"Ron?" the younger boy asked.

"Huh?" and "What?" were the only words that Ron could muster. He wasn't glad to be lying there in bed, but was relieved to have escaped from his nightmare. He gradually tuned in his brother's voice.

"I wrestle off for 135 today," Nick continued. "Dad says he can get off early enough to drive to the dual on Thursday. Do you think you'll be able to go with him?"

Ron felt the knot grow in his stomach. He wouldn't go out in public. Not for his brother, not for anybody. Fortunately, he had the perfect excuse.

"Nick, I've got rehab on Thursday."

"I know, but I thought you could re-schedule for Friday," Nick countered.

"Nick, I just had my surgery. Missing one day of rehab could be the difference between walking again and not walking. I'm sorry, Thursday won't work."

"Okay, I understand," the younger boy said, turning away and walking toward the door.

A twinge of guilt sat in Ron's stomach as he watched his younger brother leaving.

"Nick?"

His brother's voice caused Nick to stop in his tracks.

"Yeah?" he replied.

"You know you can beat Mack, right?"

"Yeah, I've beaten him twice before."

"Do it again today…but, this time, show Granger so that there is no doubt that you are the better man…because you are."

"I will," Nick replied and left Ron alone in his room.

Ron rolled back to his side and faced the wall. He closed his eyes, hoping that the nightmares wouldn't return and that he would soon wake up from the nightmare that was his life.

Chapter 52

Sean stared at the piece of paper, slowly coming to grips with its contents.

There was a B that had mysteriously moved into position among all of the A's that resided on Sean's report card. With all of the life improvements Sean had made, he was completely caught off guard by the fact that he could sober up and watch his grades fall. To most people, a B was something to be proud of or, at minimum, something readily accepted. But to Sean, after two and a half years of college, only getting A's, it was a complete disgrace.

Sean could only blame himself. He knew going into the course's final that he was on the border between an A and a B. Unfortunately for Sean, it was the final that he took the morning after staying up all night with Mandi in the hospital. Not only had he been exhausted but he had also been semi-feverish. Of course, if ruining a perfect 4.0 GPA was the price for a human life, so be it.

Otis Aamodt had tried to cheer him up by noting, "The only A's that I've ever seen on my report card are the ones in my name."

The cleverness of the comment had been amusing to Sean but not enough to make him break into a smile. He remembered back to a time in which he would have been terrified to bring home a report card with anything less than an A for fear of the wrath of his father. Now, so many years later, he had become his own harshest critic. Inability to achieve the top grade in any given subject made him a failure in his own eyes.

Chapter 53

When was the last time Nick had felt this good about the way he wrestled? The boy could not think of an answer to the question, nor did one really matter. All that mattered was his feeling of being present as he shot in for a double leg and again drove Tom Mack straight to his back.

"Two points green," Sean noted.

Nick was feeling much more aggressive than in the previous wrestle-offs as he held Mack on his back for five seconds. Finally, Nick loosened his grip and allowed the senior to turn to his stomach.

"Three points green," Sean's voice echoed in Nick's ears again.

As his opponent worked diligently to escape, Nick felt that everything was flowing just perfectly. He was in a rhythm. All of Mack's moves seemed to be in slow motion. Nick easily threaded a half nelson before Mack could get away and turned Mack to his back again. He held the senior for another three seconds before loosening his grip and allowing the older boy to struggle to his stomach.

"Two points green," Sean called again before blowing his whistle. "That's the match. Eighteen to two, a technical fall for Castle."

Nick was surprised at how quickly the match had ended. It had barely gone into the second period. Unlike the past wrestle-offs which had been fairly close, this one had been clear domination by Nick. He felt a little bad, hoping that he had not embarrassed his opponent. He was relieved to see a look of respect in Tom's eyes as the boys shook hands and Sean raised Nick's arm in the air.

"Congratulations, Nick, you're back on varsity at 135," the assistant coach proclaimed, patting the boy on the back.

Nick grinned sheepishly as he accepted his coach's remarks. He looked over to Tom who was completely exhausted.

"Tom," Sean continued, "you should be proud of the way you've been wrestling lately. If it is an option, you should think about moving to 130. I know you were a little bit light at 135."

Nick felt on top of the world as he walked with Sean to don his running shoes for the day's conditioning. He couldn't think of anything that could bring him down.

"That's the best I've seen you wrestle," Sean commended the boy again. "How is your weight?"

The question pulled Nick back to Earth. This was an area that still needed attention.

"I was 142 this morning," Nick admitted causing both himself and Sean to grimace.

"Ouch! And you've got to make scratch weight to certify."

"Yeah, I know, no meals for me."

"Nick, that's not acceptable," Sean admonished him. "You are going to eat. I'm going to watch to make sure of that. You're not going to wrestle one of the top 135-pounders in the state after having starved yourself for two days. You're already giving up two pounds to him."

Nick didn't know what to say. He just hung his head as he changed into his running shoes.

"While you are showering after practice, I'll put a meal plan together for you," Sean continued. "I expect you to follow it word for word, calorie for calorie."

Chapter 54

Nick was antsy as he stood in line waiting for the coaches to call his weight. His nervous energy alone was ten times the energy level he had felt leading up to any other 135-pound match this season.

He looked over to Coach MacCallister who was busy weighing a Jamestown wrestler. The meal plan he had provided was simple, yet it worked. Over the past few days, Nick had followed it to the letter. Along with extra time working out, the meal plan had been the key to Nick being able to have a small lunch and not have to run after school today; or even feel compelled to wear multiple layers of clothing on the bus trip.

Nick fully realized that this hadn't been an individual effort. He looked around the room at Dino, Kevin Hermanns and Colin Bradford. All three had been instrumental in the process, watching him at lunch and working with him before, during and after practice to ensure that he burned off a few extra ounces each day prior to the day of the match.

Colin in particular had joked that he was serving his own interests by making sure that Nick made weight at 135, commenting that, after the way Nick had wrestled at 140 in Colin's absence, he didn't want to give the boy any reason to move up a weight class and take his spot. Nick had to smile at the comment, keeping in mind the fact that he had felt like Colin's perpetual practice dummy as long as Nick could remember.

The coaches called the 130-pound wrestlers to the scale. Nick looked toward the back of the line and made eye contact with Dino. He knew that the big guy had been struggling with his own weight again, even with the extra two pounds. Dino's body wanted to grow to at least 225 pounds at that exact moment. The only thing holding it back was the boy's workout regimen and dedication to seeing the bar drop when the coaches put the scale at 217. "His body fat must be nothing," Nick thought as he pondered his big friend's plight.

Nick looked over to Coach MacCallister as the 135-pound wrestlers were called to the scale. "If I even hear a rumor that you are puking things back up, you will be cut from varsity forever," the man had commented as he had given Nick the meal plan days ealier.

Nick knew that bulimia was not uncommon in his sport. He admired his coach for being dedicated to ensuring that the team cut weight safely, even if he had been mildly put off by his coach's suggestion that Nick would ever consider taking such drastic measures to make weight. Nick had seen others get ridiculed even years after being caught forcing themselves to vomit in order to make weight.

Nick measured his opponent as the boy stood on the scale, made weight at 137 and stepped off again. His tension suddenly increased as he stepped on the scale and knew that all eyes would be on him.

The opposing coach watched the bar drop like a rock.

"137," the man commented, "he makes it."

"We need to certify this one at scratch weight," Granger interrupted before Nick could step off the scale.

Nick felt the hair on the back of his neck rise as the man moved the bar. The scale back in his own locker room had proclaimed the boy to be on weight. He hoped that the scale he stood on would display a similar result.

"Well, you're not light," the man commented, starting the bar at 134 pounds.

Nick held his breath as the coach moved the bar to 135 on the nose. As everyone looked on, the faintest crack of light revealed itself just above the bar, causing Nick to want to jump up and down for joy and the opposing coach to proclaim, "It breaks. Congratulations, son, you win two more pounds for the rest of the season."

He felt very proud as he watched the Jamestown coach and the referee sign his weight certification form.

Sean looked over at Nick and the two exchanged smiles. Everything was falling into place. Nick felt great and, with the ability to add two more pounds under his belt, his confidence continued to rise.

Chapter 55

Nick walked down the hall in the rehabilitation clinic. It had been several months since his dad had needed to send him in after his brother. For some reason, the clinic now had a different feel to it.

Maybe Nick shouldn't have been too surprised. Everything in Nick's life seemed to have a different feel to it these days. Since early January, nearly a month earlier, he had been wrestling well. His newfound confidence on the mat, coupled with smarter weight-cutting technique off of the mat, had put him on the winning end of most matches.

He was beginning to really enjoy practice. He found himself working with Dino as they pushed each other and the rest of the team to continually work harder and wrestle better. Several times, he had even been selected to lead the team's morning conditioning drills.

At the Capital tournament, the state's biggest event annually, Nick felt he had wrestled especially well. The tournament featured all of the state's Class A teams, several of the top Class B teams and a handful of top teams from neighboring states. Over the course of the weekend, Nick had pinned two opponents and won several other matches before being beaten out, one round shy of placing in the top six. The event had only given extra fuel to the fire inside Nick as he had watched how proudly Dino stood on top of the platform to accept his championship trophy.

One of Nick's few concerns these days was his bigger friend's weight. He was glad that there was only a month left in the season as Dino's body wanted to expand beyond the limits that his weight class allowed. While Nick felt as if he could eat double lunches on match days, he was watching his friend have to work harder and harder to see the scale's bar drop. Yet each time, without missing a beat, Dino found a way to shed the weight at the right time.

Something in Nick's winning ways seemed to be striking a chord with his coaches as well. While it had never been a surprise when Coach MacCallister had congratulated him and greeted him after a match, he was finding more and more that Coach Granger would often give him a cold nod of approval. It was more support than Nick thought he could ever hope to find from the man.

Nick rounded a corner and could hear his brother's voice in the distance. The older boy was yelling, probably rooting himself on as he cleared another hurdle in his recovery. If there was one person in the world to whom Nick still felt inferior, it was his brother. He had been noticing that, despite the inability of Ron's legs to cooperate, the boy's upper body was growing ever stronger. It made him wonder what Ron was doing in his rehab sessions.

Nick's mind was still pondering this question when he distinctly heard his brother yell, "Help!" Nick instinctively broke into a sprint as a chill ran up his spine.

Only steps away from the door to his brother's room, Nick heard a crash resonate from within the facility, immediately followed by Ron's voice, yelling every curse word imaginable.

Nick looked in the room and saw his brother sitting helplessly on the floor below two parallel bars. He had braces on his legs and his personal trainer was trying to get him into his wheelchair as Ron continued to spew vulgarity with a tone that sounded like he may break into tears any moment.

Nick ducked back behind the door before Ron could see him. He knew that his older brother would be mortified if he knew that Nick had witnessed him in such a weakened state. He waited for several minutes that seemed like an eternity as Ron's yelling eventually tapered off and then waited a few more for good measure. It wasn't until he was sure that his brother had regained his composure that Nick allowed himself to enter the room and retrieve his sibling.

Chapter 56

I'M NOT GOING TO LOSE THIS MATCH!"

Nick's own words rang in his ears as he returned to the center of the mat. Why would he say such words? Why did he believe them?

Fifteen minutes ago, it would have made sense that he would believe them. Through the month of January and into early February, life had treated the boy well. In fact, up until the start of this match, he had been wrestling better than he ever had before.

Since returning to his slot at 135 pounds, Nick had gone fourteen and six. He had gotten to a point at which he was wrestling with Hermanns at practice nearly every day and giving the boy a good match. Who would have thought that he would match so closely with a 145-pounder ranked third in the state? Beyond that, there had even been a few times when Nick had wrestled Vassec and taken the highly-ranked 152-pounder down.

His weight was under control, his technique was sound and he was feeling strong. His confidence had started to spill out beyond the mat. There were even a couple of girls in the school that Oscar said were taking notice of him.

"I'M NOT GOING TO LOSE THIS MATCH!"

The statement would have made perfect sense last Saturday. He would have believed it and would have been right in saying it in any match other than the semifinal. That match had seen him lose in overtime to one of the top-ranked wrestlers in a neighboring state, earning a black-eye in the process. It was the only match he had lost in two weeks as, subsequently, Nick pinned two opponents on his way to placing third in that tournament. He had felt proud while standing on the platform, receiving his medal. But more than that, he was hungry, hungry to redeem that loss and get back onto the mat.

Coming into tonight's dual, he had the world on a string. He had looked forward to his re-match with Tony Heidt, the state's second-ranked 135-pounder. Nick felt ready to redeem himself for a December showing in which he had been dragged from one side of the mat to the other and back again before the senior finally showed mercy and pinned him.

His optimism had ended about ten seconds into the first period when Heidt took him down, put him on his back and held him within an inch of being pinned for thirty seconds. The rest of the first period had not gone any better, nor had the second. A bloody nose had sent Nick back to his corner down by a score of fifteen to three.

As glad as he had been to get away from Heidt for a few minutes, he had not been so happy to face Coach Granger. For the first time in a month, the angry look was back in his eyes as he stuffed cotton into Nick's nose and complained about the Castle family's propensity toward bleeding. Encouraging words from Coach MacCallister had just fanned the flames as the head coach then went into a tirade about how the team couldn't afford to give up a pin or a technical fall in this match if they hoped to win the dual.

As if Nick weren't frustrated enough with his own performance, listening to Granger brought the boy's blood to near boiling. Yes, he knew that Vassec was out with an injury and that the rest of them had to make up that ground. He certainly didn't need to be belittled with this reminder. It was at that point that Nick snapped. Forget trying to avoid being pinned. Forget trying to avoid being put on his back again, which would result in the points Heidt needed for a technical fall. Looking his coach square in the eye, he declared, "I'M NOT GOING TO LOSE THIS MATCH!"

Why did he say it? Why did he believe it?

As he returned to the center of the mat and got into referee's position, everything around him disappeared. He didn't hear his teammates. He didn't see the crowd. He had moved to a place in which all that existed was in the confines of the mat.

"Top man on." The words came from somewhere near him as he felt his opponent mount. "Ready… wrestle."

Nick burst forward as Heidt held on. The older boy tried to gain hand control but Nick sat out. Heidt chin-dropped Nick to the mat but Nick rolled through and avoided any near-fall points.

On his belly again, Nick began scrambling toward his hands and knees. As Heidt tried to turn him, Nick sat out once again. This time, as Heidt reached around for hand control, Nick used his opponent's own hands as leverage and turned to face the boy, gaining an escape and a point just prior to the foghorn sounding to end the second period.

Did Heidt feel the tide turning? If he did, he certainly didn't show it as he claimed, "You're mine, Castle."

Nick met the comment with a cold stare.

Heidt had his choice of position in the third period and chose neutral. As the whistle blew to begin the period, Nick shot at Heidt's legs. As the older boy sprawled, Nick kept moving forward as his opponent pushed his head toward the mat. As Nick tried to rotate out, Heidt shucked him by and rotated behind for the takedown and two more points before the boys rolled off the mat.

It did register with Nick that Heidt was only two points away from winning the match by technical fall. As the two moved back to the center of the mat, Nick continued to stare the boy down as he asked Nick whether he preferred to be pinned or lose by technical fall.

The entire process of getting back to the center of the mat, getting into position, Heidt mounting and the referee saying "Ready..." was a blur. All that registered was the word, "Wrestle."

In an instant, Nick resumed crawling forward toward an escape. Arriving on his feet, he felt Heidt trying to get his hands clasped at approximately Nick's waist. In a single fluid motion, Nick separated Heidt's hands, rotated his hips to the left and executed a fireman's carry, using Heidt's momentum to bring him to the mat. Before Heidt could react, Nick had transferred his hold to an under-hook and put the boy in a head and arm lock, squeezing it tight.

Nick didn't hear the crowd or his teammates. He only heard the voices of MacCallister and Granger yelling, "Go toward his head! Go toward his head!" and he complied. Grasping the head and arm lock tighter and tighter, Nick maneuvered toward Heidt's head, putting all of his weight on the boy's chest.

Hearing the ref count for near-fall, Nick's neck veins began to show as he grasped the hold even tighter and his opponent turned red. No sounds around him registered. For Nick, there was complete silence until he heard the ref slap the mat.

The slap brought Nick back to the room. He let his world again expand beyond the mat as he now heard the Riverside crowd and team go wild. He let go of his grip and looked around in amazement.

Why had he said those words? Why had he believed them? Nick did not stop to ponder the questions. He walked back to the center of the mat and had his hand raised in victory.

* * *

Nick sat beside the match, watching intently as Brian Keaton left the mat in defeat, dropping Riverside's lead to a one-point margin. With only two matches remaining they still had an opportunity to win.

He watched Dino on the warm-up mat, preparing himself for one of the only 215-pound wrestlers in the state who many thought could beat him. By all accounts, this should be a close match. Dino had only won by a single point the last time these two had faced each other. It was a time when Riverside needed six points from a pin from Dino as Clifford Vassec's opponent at heavyweight had already pinned Clifford twice this season.

'Indestructible' was the only word that echoed through Nick's mind as he watched his big friend saunter toward the mat. Nick turned his attention to Dino's opponent, Billy Danvers, and thought he noted fear in his eyes as Dino intensely approached the center of the mat, mechanically snapping his headgear without taking his eyes off of his opponent.

Nick felt as if it were a showdown in the old west. As the referee blew the whistle, the two wrestlers moved into position. Danvers, a strong kid in his own right, tried to overpower Dino but it was clear that Benz was the stronger of the two boys as he completely manhandled his opponent and pushed him off the mat, causing the ref to blow his whistle.

As Dino walked back to the center of the mat, Nick could see Coach Granger making some kind of a motion. Dino only nodded.

The referee blew his whistle again, re-starting the match. This time, Danvers decided to take a new approach and shot on Dino immediately. Dino sprawled, jammed Danvers' head into the mat and spun around behind the boy to earn his two points.

"Indestructible," Nick thought again. He didn't know Danvers' exact ranking in the state but knew that it was in the top four. Yet, somehow, Dino made everything look easy.

There was a cold intensity in Dino's eyes as he put in his legs and began cranking on a half nelson.

In unison with Granger's cry of, "We need a pin," Danvers buckled under Dino's strength turning to his back.

Dino's expression was stoic as he continued to apply pressure. His opponent's face turned red as he fought in vain to avoid being pinned but found that his own strength and will were not enough. This highly ranked wrestler collapsed under Dino's power, dropping his shoulders flat against the mat. The referee slapped the mat, signaling the pin.

"Indestructible," Nick thought a third time as he watched Dino having his arm raised in victory. Tonight had gone very well for the team.

Despite Nick's own performance in pinning Heidt tonight, he believed that Dino in particular deserved to be praised for his contributions.

Chapter 57

Nick's body walked into the school but his mind was still far away. It was well before noon but Nick felt like he had already put in a full day.

The entire Castle family had arrived at the hospital around 6:30 a.m. This was the big day. Ron was having his final surgery, which had the potential to allow him to get feeling back in his legs. The doctors had explained something about the spinal cord and some nerves but it had all gone right over Nick's head. All he really knew was that Ron was excited about it but it scared their mom to death.

She had kissed Ron on the cheek before he was rolled into the operating room and had insisted on staying at the hospital while Nick's dad brought him to school. Nick wanted to stay as well but both parents believed that the best place for him was in school, where he could get his mind off of his brother being under the knife. For whatever reason, Nick didn't think it mattered where he was that morning; his mind would remain with his brother.

The boy hurried down the empty hall. He was late but at least he had his permission slip. His parents had secured it for him the day before. It was getting close to 10:30 which meant that he had to walk into Mr. Garrett's Biology class late. Why did the timing have to be such that he disrupted a class in which Todd Johnson sat right in front of him?

Perhaps it wouldn't be so bad. Since their Gym class wrestling match over a month earlier, Todd had done nothing more than give Nick dirty looks. He mostly ignored the boy which was completely alright with Nick. Yet, for whatever reason, there was still fear that he was going to walk into the class and become the center of attention due to one of the bully's rude comments.

Nick power-walked around the corner and nearly flattened a girl coming out of the restroom. She looked him right in the eye as he tried to make his way around her. He instantly turned red.

"Hi Nick," she said.

"Hi…Hi Sandi," Nick stuttered.

His mind suddenly was in a fog, no longer dwelling on his brother. A really pretty girl had just spoken to him. What should he do? His heart suddenly raced and he felt like he was going to break into a sweat.

"Are you coming to school late today?" Sandi asked, taking a few strides at a fast pace to keep up with him.

"What should I do?" Nick thought. "She's walking with me." His first instinct told him that walking fast was bound to be rude so he slowed to a more manageable pace, one that would allow her to easily keep up with him.

"Yeah, how did you know?" he finally replied.

"You're wearing your jacket," Sandi responded.

Nick felt like he was turning five shades of red. How could he have missed something that obvious? Yet it had allowed him to remain in the conversation. It didn't look like she was giving up on him either so something must be going right.

"Oh," Nick said, laughing nervously. "I guess that would be a giveaway."

They walked a bit further in silence, causing Nick to get even more nervous. Why couldn't he think of anything to say? Finally, he blurted out the only thing that came to mind.

"My brother Ron has another surgery today. They removed a blockage in his spine in early January and now they've got to do some touch-ups."

Sandi looked concerned. Nick didn't want to upset her but was pleased that she seemed interested in the conversation.

"Do you know anything about neurology?" Nick asked.

Sandi just shook her head, 'no'.

"I don't really either," Nick continued. "We went to be with Ron until they took him into the operating room. Mom and Dad thought I should come to school to keep my mind off of it."

Nick reached his locker and stopped. To his surprise, Sandi waited for him as he put his jacket inside and grabbed his books.

"What class are you going to?" she asked.

"Biology," Nick responded. He was very glad that she was taking the lead in finding a new topic.

"Mr. Garrett?" she prodded.

"Yeah, I'm not sure if he likes me."

"Why?" she asked.

"He told me, 'Nick, I don't want you to fall asleep in my class today. You drool and it's really gross.'"

As soon as the words left his mouth, Nick was mortified at what he had just said. Who would say something like that and expect a girl to stay the least bit interested. "What kind of an idiot am I?" Nick thought as Sandi gave him a 'that's gross' look.

"But I don't drool," Nick quickly mentioned, trying to recover but not being all that sure whether he was succeeding as he stammered his way through further explanation. "He was just making that up. He just doesn't want me to sleep in his class...and I wouldn't...if I could help it. I just fall asleep... sometimes...that's all."

Sandi stopped suddenly. Nick's blood ran cold. Now he had done it. Not only was she mortified that he had talked about drool, she wasn't going to walk with him anymore. She'd probably tell all of her friends what a dork he was. Surely he would never get to talk to a pretty girl again.

"This is my class," Sandi mentioned, pointing at a closed classroom door.

Nick paused briefly, trying to think of something intelligent to say.

"I'll see you in French class?" he asked.

"Oui, Monsieur," she confirmed. Then, she broke into a big, beautiful smile and continued, "Maybe we could even be partners for some of the conversations today?"

Nick could only smile back and nod as Sandi turned to walk into her classroom. He knew that he must be blushing but he also knew that he had just talked to a very pretty girl and, seeing as she wanted to talk to him again, he must have done fairly well at it.

* * *

Nick opened the door as quietly as possible. His seat was only two rows from the back of the room. If he was lucky, nobody would even notice his entrance with the exception of Mr. Garrett who already expected him to be late.

The doorknob made very little noise, bolstering the youth's faith that his plan to join the class undetected was going to work. He entered, shut the door quietly and then turned to look in horror as Mr. Garrett stopped his lecture mid-sentence. The teacher, along with everyone else in the room, turned their eyes to stare at Nick.

The boy suddenly felt sick. He really didn't want to deal with this right now, or ever for that matter. Finding a way to divert their attention to something else was the only thing on Nick's mind as he began to pull out his excused absence slip.

His fingers fumbled as they dug for the slip. He was overcome with confusion as he watched his teacher slowly begin clapping.

Nick's confusion continued to grow as he noted that the other students, one at a time began clapping in unison with Mr. Garrett.

Suddenly, Nick realized that the projection on the wall, which had read something about plant cell biology when he had entered the room, now read, "Congratulations, Nick!!!"

Nick began to blush as he tried to figure out what was going on.

"What?" he finally asked.

"Don't you work for the *Herald*?" the teacher asked, referring to the city's daily newspaper.

"Yes," Nick replied, still trying to find some rhyme or reason as to why that would be a reason to put him on a pedestal.

"Did you read this morning's edition?"

Reading the newspaper had been the furthest thing from Nick's mind this particular morning. He and Chewie had barely had time to deliver the darn things before accompanying Ron to the hospital.

"No," Nick finally answered, "we took my brother in for surgery."

Without missing a beat, the teacher responded, "Luckily, I have a copy here," pulled open the sports section and began reading.

"Athletes of the week, wrestling: Riverside's Nick Castle, a sophomore, appears to be following in the footsteps of his older brother and gaining momentum in the weeks leading to the conference tournament. In the last week, Nick placed third in a competitive out-of-state tournament, then returned to pin our state's second-ranked wrestler, a feat that enabled Riverside to win its dual."

Nick felt like his face was on fire as the class continued to watch him.

"According to Coach Granger," Mr. Garrett continued, "the kid who beat you in the semi-finals in that recent tournament was one of the top wrestlers in his state. I would say that you're doing very well. Congratulations."

"Thanks," Nick replied as he settled into his seat. While flattered by the recognition of his accomplishments, Nick was relieved to hear the teacher turn the subject back to Biology so that he could step out of the spotlight. He was still a bit jittery as he situated his notebook on his desk and nearly jumped as a large hand suddenly came down on top of it.

Nick looked up to see what he suspected. The hand belonged to Todd Johnson who was sitting in his seat, staring at Nick. Nick felt his own hand slowly tightening into a fist under the desk as he stared Todd in the eye for a moment before the larger boy could speak.

"Congratulations, Castle, you did good. Keep it up," Todd finally uttered quietly. He looked Nick in the eye for only another moment before turning back to pay attention to the lecture.

Nick was confused and felt as if his eyes were about to mist over.

"Thanks," was the only word that he could find to whisper in reply.

Chapter 58

Sean drove slowly away from the airport. A lighter car would have been thrown around by the strong winds but his Galaxie 500 stood her ground.

It was too early in the morning to be out and about on such a bitterly cold February day but Randy had needed a ride in order to make it to his 7:45 flight and Sean was quick to volunteer his taxi service.

Sean thought of the test that he should be studying for. He had gotten his first B the prior semester thanks to staying up all night with Mandi instead of studying for his Physics 305 final. He promised himself that giving Randy this ride would not yield the same result on this first Physics 306 test of the semester.

The roads were slick. Snow was starting to fall and would act as an abrasive to the ice already on the roads but would also reduce visibility. In the end, it would be about an even trade from a driving speed standpoint.

Sean's mind wandered as he listened to Jimmy Buffett. In the distance he saw tail lights in the ditch and made a mental note to be especially careful around that point in the road. He decreased his speed while keeping an eye out for the slick spot which had caused the motorist to lose control.

From Sean's point of view, the road wasn't any worse at that spot than at any other juncture on the highway. He took a moment to watch the poor sap in the ditch, trying in vain to move his half-buried vehicle. Judging by the looks of the man, he must be from somewhere warm. He wore only a light overcoat over his stylish suit with no hat, gloves or scarf.

Considering the bleak scene for a moment, Sean drove only a few hundred feet more before pulling over to the shoulder of the road and backing up to offer some help. Frostbite struck quickly and, from the looks of the guy, he could soon become a winter road hazard death statistic.

By the time Sean returned to the spot in the road where the man had veered off, the guy was anxiously waving at him. The man ducked back into his car to retrieve a briefcase before trudging through knee-deep snow on his way to Sean's car.

"Can I give you some help?" Sean asked as the man opened the door.

"Yes, please," the man answered, getting into Sean's passenger seat. His face and hands were beet red and his attire, which Sean guessed had looked very professional upon arrival at the airport, was now wrinkled and sloppy wet.

"Can you help me push this out?" the man inquired.

Sean tried not to smile as he looked at the car. It had dug a deep trench in the snow on its way into the ditch.

"You're in pretty deep," Sean replied, shaking his head. "It'll take a tow truck or a Steiger to pull that out."

The man gave him a confused look, obviously knowing nothing about what a Steiger was or likely, nothing about tractors in general.

"I've got to be at McCannel Hall by 8:30, is that far from here?" the man asked, changing the subject.

"I can have you there in about fifteen minutes if you don't mind leaving your car," Sean replied. Then, reading the man's expression, he continued, "It's not like anybody is going to be able to take off with it."

The man seemed as anxious to talk as he was grateful to have someone pick him up. Sean learned that his name was Larry Darkins and he was in town from Dallas, recruiting Accounting students. Much of the man's life story flew right over Sean's head as he concentrated on keeping his car on the road and was distracted by thoughts of how unprepared he suddenly felt for this morning's test.

As the conversation moved to classic Fords, they found some common ground in their love for Mustangs. Larry had a 1966 convertible, Sean's dream car, but certainly not practical this time of year in this climate.

Sean liked the man and ended up giving him the phone number of his buddy, Dudley, at a service station not far from the highway. While Sean hated to hand the favor that Dudley owed him over to a stranger, for some reason, it felt like the right thing to do.

Larry seemed mildly impressed by Sean's connections and his ability to get things done, even commenting that, if Sean were an Accounting major, he would save himself a day of interviews and just give the job he had to offer over to Sean.

The comment made Sean smile. Even if this excursion cost him his Physics grade, at least it earned him a promising career as an accountant. "If you're good to people, they'll be good to you," Sean thought as he dropped the man off at McCannel Hall.

Shaking Larry's hand and driving toward home, Sean hoped that this extra outing had not cost him too much study time.

Chapter 59

Nick made his way through the maze of narrow hallways that comprised the music and theater section of the high school. He had participated in a few summer theater programs there in elementary school and sometimes enjoyed re-living those memories by taking the long way through the department.

He knew that he could never do well in theater or music. Being the center of attention and having to look out at a room of people staring at him scared the daylights out of him. Even if it didn't, Ron had drawn a firm line for him one day stating that a person can be an athlete or a thespian but not both. For whatever reason, Nick had believed him and spent very little time in that part of the building.

A familiar voice caught Nick's ear as he passed the choir room door, causing him to stop in his tracks and peek inside. There, talking to the choir director stood Dino. What in the world could the big guy be doing in this setting?

"You would be good in this part," the man told Dino. "I really think you should give it a try."

"Thanks, I'll think about it," Dino responded as he took some kind of book from the man and began walking away, right toward Nick.

Nick turned red, knowing that he was busted. Then, surprisingly, he saw the same look on Dino's face that he felt he had on his own.

"So do you have some kind of comment, smart guy?"

Nick was surprised that his friend came after him so harshly.

"About what?" Nick asked innocently.

Dino looked frustrated, as if Nick were playing a game with him.

"About the school musical," Dino replied.

The cat was out of the bag. The big guy was making the leap, bridging the gap between the jocks and the drama pack. Why on earth would he venture into this uncharted territory? In a couple of weeks, he would surely be a state wrestling champion. Wasn't that enough? What more could a person want?

"You're trying out?" Nick asked, knowing the answer full well.

"I don't know," Dino replied.

Nick had never seen his friend like this before. Dino was clearly self-conscious about the whole situation. As he looked back into the choir room, Nick followed his gaze, noticing that it fell on Cheri Winters who was now talking to the choir director.

Everything was suddenly clear. This was all just another way for Dino to get close to Cheri. Nick wasn't sure if he admired his friend for continually coming up with new ways to woo the girl or pitied him for being such a glutton for punishment. He had seen Dino carrying Cheri's books a week earlier. She seemed to be fine with the fact that Dino was shouldering her load but didn't seem to pay a whole lot of attention to him while he was doing so.

It only took Nick a split second to make his decision on this matter.

"Why wouldn't you?" Nick asked, trying to sound encouraging. He made the choice right there that he would support his friend no matter what.

"I tried out for *The Pajama Game* last year and your brother wouldn't let me hear the end of it," Dino responded. "I sang the song, *Racing with the Clock* for my audition and for the next month, every time I saw Ron, he would sing, 'When you're racing with the clock, Benzy wants to be a theater jock.' I should have smacked him."

Nick couldn't help but laugh a little, thinking of his brother's clever wit.

"You'll be laughing with my knee in your butt in a minute," the big guy threatened.

"I'm sorry man, it's just kind of funny," Nick responded. "I just can't see you reciting Shakespeare."

"I'm not going to be reciting Shakespeare. It's a musical, *Oklahoma.*"

"So you'll be singing?" Nick asked.

The younger boy found this even more humorous but painfully held back his smile, knowing that Dino would be increasingly annoyed.

"Yes, a song called *Lonely Room.*"

"You are really interested in this?" Nick confirmed.

"Yeah."

"Ron would never let me live it down if I tried to be in theater. But I know you'll do well in the show. I'll even come and see you if you want me to."

Dino looked back and saw Cheri emerging from the choir room. He waved to her. To Nick's surprise, she waved back and smiled. Could it be that Nick was wrong about this relationship? Did Dino actually have a chance? Maybe the guy was indestructible on multiple fronts?

"Have you asked Cheri out?" Nick asked.

"No, I haven't asked her yet. I'm waiting until after state. I think she'd like to go out with a state champion."

The two continued to walk toward the locker room, not saying anything for a long while. Dino shoved the script book into his book bag, wanting it to be well hidden before he entered the athletes' territory.

The two boys looked at each other briefly, passing a moment of mutual understanding and respect.

"Good luck on the audition," Nick whispered. "You'll do great."

"Thanks," Dino replied.

Dino opened the locker room door and the two boys entered, leaving the non-wrestling world behind for another few hours.

Chapter 60

Sean was eight shades of tired as he slipped into bed. He had stayed up far later than he had planned, spending most of the evening watching Kelly's TV and talking with Otis. It was nearly bar closing time so Sean was happy to be getting to bed before Kelly and others returned, inevitably keeping him up for several more hours.

He pondered his recent Physics 306 exam for a moment. Although he wouldn't get his results for another week, he didn't feel that it had gone very well. The last thing he needed was for his grades to start slipping the semester before he would go through on-campus recruiting. He promised himself to redouble his efforts in the class the remainder of the school year.

Next, the young man thought ahead to the following day's conference tournament. He was worried about Dino's weight but had promised to let the big guy into the school at 6:30 the next morning to shed whatever excess weight he had. Once Dino did so, he was the team's one sure-thing for a conference champion.

Sean's mind wandered a bit more through the line-up as he crawled between the sheets. Joel Vassec and Hermanns would be seeded number one or two in their respective weight classes. Either of them could pull in a championship without surprising anyone.

"What about Castle?" Sean wondered as he tried to get comfortable. The sophomore was certainly a dark horse but had the heart, talent and now the confidence to win. Nick was essentially Sean's protégé so the young man had a soft spot for him. With his newfound self-assurance, he could be hard to stop.

Sean was just beginning to say his prayers when the phone rang.

"Great," the young man thought, sarcastically, "someone needs a ride."

He pondered rolling over and pulling a pillow over his head but the wind howling outside his window changed his mind. The temperature was well below zero. He couldn't let his friends walk home in that kind of weather. He knew that he would never forgive himself if Kelly or one of his other friends got frostbite or worse. People had died of exposure in warmer temperatures than tonight's.

Reluctantly, he crossed the room and picked up the phone an instant before it would have gone to voicemail. Loud music blared in his ear, causing him to have to shout, "Hello!"

"Mac," the voice came back on the other end.

Sean froze. It wasn't Kelly's voice or that of any other Beta Beta Beta. The young man's spine tingled as he realized that it was Mandi.

He pondered hanging up on her, but opted to hear her out. "Hey," was his only response.

"Mac, you've gotta come get us," the young woman continued, slurring her words.

Sean's frustration rose as he looked at his clock which showed a time of 12:23. He had to be up in five and a half hours. The last thing in the world that he needed was to venture out into the cold and end up babysitting Mandi.

"Actually, Mandi, I was just about to go to bed. Don't you have a designated driver?"

He didn't even need to ask that question. Responsibility wasn't Mandi's strong point. In fact, he would be surprised if she had even worn a coat. Fashion often took precedence over common sense.

"He left us," she continued. "You need to come now, it's freezing out there. It's like 40 below."

Sean was perturbed as he considered his options. He was sure that he wouldn't be able to sleep if he didn't go get her. Yet, at the same time, she was still among the people that he least wanted to see. He finally gave in and asked the question.

"Where are you at?"

"The Rock."

"How many people are there with you?"

"Just me and Angie."

Sean paused for a moment. It would be a royal pain to pick her up, drive her across town and get back home to bed. He was sure that it would cost him at least another hour of sleep. If he overslept and wasn't at the high school promptly at 6:30, he would never forgive himself. Yet, he couldn't leave Mandi and Angie to the elements either. Reluctantly, he agreed.

"I'll be there as soon as I can. Can you wait by the back door?"

There was no reply. Perhaps she hadn't heard him? The music was still very loud in the background.

"Mandi?" he reiterated a bit louder.

"Yeah," came the reply, then the line went dead as she hung up the phone.

Sean hung up as well, thinking that a "Thank you" would have been appropriate. Then again, he had come to expect far less from this woman.

He slipped into jeans and a sweatshirt, the whole time pondering how much he hated The Rock. It was one of those bars that had music so loud that a guy could hardly hear himself think, much less hear what anyone around him was saying. None of his friends went there either. This would be a quick in and out since he didn't have to be concerned about getting into a long conversation with any of his classmates.

If he was lucky, maybe he could make the round trip in 45 minutes. Could he possibly catch a little sleep while Dino was cutting weight? He continued thinking of extra rationale for making the trip as he donned his coat and headed out into the frigid night.

Chapter 61

Nick couldn't sleep. It was approaching 1:00 a.m. and he had more energy than he could fathom.

All he could think about was the upcoming Conference tournament. He knew he had been seeded third but, for whatever reason, he felt like his first high school tournament title was looming. Being named "Wrestler of the Week" by the local newspaper had just been icing on the cake. Nick felt like a machine every time he stepped onto the mat these days. He had even gone as far as to tell his brother that, over the past few weeks, he had felt like he was unbeatable.

Ron had seemed almost proud of Nick during the conversation and Nick had used the opportunity to ask Ron to come to the tournament. To his surprise, Ron had agreed to do so, under the condition that Nick promise to win the championship.

After a lot of hemming and hawing, Nick had finally blurted out the words, "I promise I'll win the conference tournament if you will come and watch."

Now, lying in bed, he couldn't believe that he had said those words. A brief chill ran up his spine. The chill disappeared again as he whispered the words quietly to himself.

"I promise I'll win the conference tournament."

It wasn't such a hard phrase to say. What surprised Nick was that he had said it. In particular, he was downright astonished that he had said it to his brother.

Nick was so full of energy, he just wanted to get up and run or work out or something... He didn't even know what. He just wanted the tournament to be here. He wanted his opponents to be on the mat now so that he could defeat them before this feeling of being superhuman disappeared.

He watched the clock turn to 12:55 as he rolled over and hugged his pillow. The morning would come soon enough; he could hardly wait for it to arrive.

Chapter 62

Sean sat quietly, staring at The Rock's entrance and waiting for Mandi to come out.

How long had he been waiting? It had to have been at least fifteen to twenty minutes. Or maybe it just seemed that long as he listened to the wind howling outside. He was beginning to get irritated.

The small digital clock affixed to his dashboard changed to 12:57.

"Come on Mandi!!!" he said to himself as he turned off the car and pulled his coat tightly around him. As he opened the door, he realized that the coat didn't help. The icy wind cut right through it as Sean sprinted toward the bar. Opening the door, he ran squarely into a very large man.

Irritated, the man looked down on him.

"We're closed," he said. "Nobody else comes in."

Sean peered around the darkened room, hoping to see Mandi quickly.

"I've just come to pick up some friends," he explained.

The bouncer continued to study him with a stone-cold gaze.

"You've got two minutes. Find your friends and all of you get out of my bar. Some of us have families waiting for us."

Heeding the bouncer's words, Sean took four quick steps into the bar before being stopped in his tracks by a strong hand grasping his shoulder. He wheeled around, expecting to see the bouncer and came face to face with Cole Tyler.

"Oh, it's you," Sean commented.

Cole gazed coolly across the bar to the pool tables. "You're not going to cause any trouble, are you? The bouncer is a friend of mine."

Sean followed Cole's gaze, quickly finding the source of Cole's concern. Kevin Lakes was standing with a group of friends, drinking and watching a buddy finish a game of eight-ball.

"Great," Sean muttered under his breath.

"No, I'm just here to pick up a friend. Hopefully I'll be out of here before they notice me."

"Okay," Cole replied, letting Sean go.

Looking in the opposite direction from the pool tables, Sean was happy to find Angie leaning on the bar, talking to the bartender. He quickly made his way to her.

"Where is Mandi?" he asked.

Angie seemed confused. "What? What are you doing here?"

Sean felt the hair on the back of his neck bristle. He was already tired and needed to get up in a few hours the way it was. He didn't have time for this.

"Mandi asked me to pick you and her up at the back door. Where is she?"

Angie still looked confused. "Sean, she left with some guy half an hour ago."

"WHAT?!!!!" Sean didn't know who he was more angry at, Mandi for calling him and leaving or himself for, once again, letting himself get into this situation.

"She told me that I'd need to find my own ride," Angie continued. "Dave, my favorite bartender, is going to give me a lift."

Sean just looked on in amazement. "She really left?"

"Yeah, a while ago." It was clear that Angie felt bad. "I'm sorry, Sean."

Sean cursed under his breath as he turned and started toward the door.

"Sean!"

Angie's voice, screaming his name, was the last thing that Sean heard clearly and was followed an instant later by an excruciating pain on the left side of his head. In the subsequent fogginess there was Kevin Lakes' face, a pain in his ribs and a sharp pain in his back before all went black.

Chapter 63

The buzzing was what Sean noticed first. What was that buzzing? And why did he feel so good?

There was a bright light that was very blurry, a woman's voice and a man's voice. Was he dead? What was that movie line, "Don't go into the light"? He didn't feel like he could move toward or away from the light at this point and, for whatever reason, he didn't even care.

Lost in a fog, Sean began his process of trying to focus. Where was he? Was he drunk? He sure felt drunk. Why had he started drinking again? Where was he? He sure felt good. The fog intensified and everything faded to black again.

Chapter 64

Come on, MacCallister, where are you?!!!" Dino screamed the words out loud as he slammed his hands against the steering wheel.

Nick sat quietly in the passenger's seat. The two had been waiting in Dino's car in the Riverside High School parking lot since 6:30 that morning for Sean to open the doors. Nick had only shown up for moral support but Dino needed to run and needed to do it now! The car's heater was cranked as high as it could go, but both boys doubted that temperature alone would melt away Dino's excess weight.

The 215-pounder was clearly nervous for the first time in a long time as he looked anxiously at his watch. It was after 7:45. He slammed his hands on the steering wheel again in frustration. Where was Coach MacCallister?

Nick made a mental note of the fact that this was the first time in a long time Dino had talked for an hour without mentioning Cheri. Around 6:30, Dino had mentioned her, noting that he had visited her at A'Romano's Pizza the night before and she actually seemed interested in the upcoming Conference tournament. He had promised to bring his championship medal over and show it to her after the finals. Nick was sure that the big guy's blood would run cold if it dawned on him that if he didn't make weight, there would be no tournament, championship or medal for him. Not placing at the Conference tournament meant not qualifying for the State tournament. Everything would be lost.

The boys had already talked through options. Dino could drive across town and try to run off the weight at South High School but then he would need to find a way to get back here to pick up his singlet and warm-ups before the tournament started. Then again, if he didn't make weight, he would have little need for his wrestling attire. The bigger issue was that his workout clothes were locked in his locker inside the locked building he could see through the windshield.

Driving to South was the immediate plan as it appeared to be the only option. Dino would have to run in his jeans and sweater but at least he would be running. He placed his car in gear a moment before noticing a second car pulling into the lot. It wasn't MacCallister's old beater but it did provide a light ray of hope. The window rolled down to display Granger's weathered face.

"Coach?" Dino started, "Where is Coach MacCallister? He was supposed to let me in to run at 6:30."

The head coach's voice was measured in his reply. "I just got a call from one of the university coaches. MacCallister was taken to the emergency room last night. Let's get you inside to shed that weight."

Nick was startled by Granger's words and took them with mixed feelings. He was worried about Coach MacCallister yet elated that Dino was going to get to run. Dino shut his car off and followed Granger into the school.

Nick prayed silently for MacCallister's well-being and that there was enough time for Dino to get down to his required weight.

Chapter 65

Nick's spirits climbed as the bar dropped.

"Half pound under!" the boy yelled and then let out a victorious whooping sound, slapping a high-five to Kevin Hermanns as he jumped off the scale.

Nick felt like a million bucks. He really believed the promise he had made to his brother. How could anyone possibly come close to beating him right now? He wished that he could step on the mat against the state's top ranked wrestler right this instant. Nick was ready for anybody and everybody.

"Whoo!!!" he howled again as he slapped Oscar's hand.

The little guy had a spring in his step as well as he stepped onto the scale. "Three-quarters under!!!" Oscar announced to the world as he did a victory dance on the scale's pad.

The sophomore's joy was short lived as Joel Vassec suddenly appeared behind him, snapping him in the butt with a wet towel. The towel's cracking sound could be heard across the locker room. As Oscar jumped forward in pain, he slammed into the mechanical workings of the scale, driving it into the wall.

"Hey chicken legs," the senior sneered and laughed as Oscar recoiled from the pain. "Save some of that dancing energy for when you step on the mat. You might actually win a match."

"You piece of crap!!!" Oscar yelled, tears welling up in his eyes. His mood had gone from rosy to fretful with a single snap of a towel. One that was sure to leave a mark.

Granger entered the locker room, with his usual unpleasant disposition. "Get dressed now and get over to South," he directed. "Weigh in ends in an hour."

As the boys scrambled to get dressed and pack their gear, the coach surveyed the room. "Where is Benz?" he eventually asked.

"He's upstairs running," Nick replied.

"Go up and get him, he's running out of time."

Nick pulled on his sweatshirt as he left the locker room. He knew that Dino had been about a pound over when he arrived that morning. Surely the senior would cut the weight again. Nick's main concern was whether or not the time allotted for doing so would be enough. He wanted to see Dino at the top of the platform after the state tournament. In order to get there, he would need to wrestle today.

"How is it going, Benzy?" Nick asked upon entering the wrestling room.

"I'm sweating pretty well. I'll make it," Dino replied. He seemed a bit down, rightfully so given his precarious situation.

"Do you want me to jump rope with you?"

"That's all right. By the time you got changed and got back up here, I'd be at a point at which I should stop and weigh-in anyway."

"Good," Nick responded. "Granger says we need to get over to South now."

Dino quit jumping and began toweling the river of sweat off of his face. Nick was concerned about whether or not the abbreviated workout would be enough. He had come this far down the road with his friend, he wanted them to finish the season strong together.

"I'll see you at South," Dino commented as Nick turned and made his way down the stairs.

* * *

Dino stepped on the scale and set it to 217. To his amazement, the bar dropped. His face lit up in a grin of pleasant surprise as he moved the weight to 216 and three quarters. The bar dropped again and then rose, breaking a hair below the top metal on the scale.

Granger walked in from the coaches' office, glad to see Dino's wry smile.

"Are you close?" the coach asked.

"I'm a quarter pound under," the wrestler responded.

"Shut up, how can that be possible?" Granger exclaimed in surprise. "Did you do something to the scale?"

"Serious," Dino responded. "It breaks at 216 and three quarters. When I weighed in this morning, this same scale had me over weight by a pound."

Granger looked at the scale, confirming what his wrestler was seeing. It didn't make sense but, then again, none of the other wrestlers had mentioned feeling that the thing had suddenly gone light.

"How do you feel?" the man asked.

"Like a filthy animal," Dino replied.

"A filthy animal that made weight," Granger corrected him. "Go shower up and get over there. Weigh-in ends in 45 minutes."

Dino moved all of the weights to zero, then stepped off and walked quickly toward the showers. He failed to notice that, once set to zero, the bar rested on the bottom of the bracket, an unfortunate result of Joel and Oscar's earlier horseplay.

Chapter 66

Was there supposed to be a beep? Sean thought he had heard one a while ago. Why was it that he hadn't cared then but cared now?

The fog was beginning to lift again. How many times had that happened? He heard the voices again. Off in the distance, there were male voices this time. Where was he? Was it weird that he didn't care?

Sean tried to stretch but stopped when his ribs hurt. Why did his ribs hurt? Oddly, he didn't care about that either.

"Focus, MacCallister, focus!" He thought.

The voices were there again. They were closer this time. There were multiple male voices. What were they saying? Were they talking about him?

"Focus!"

Where were those voices coming from? Why weren't his eyes open? Why hadn't it occurred to him before that he should open his eyes?

"Ow!"

His left eye was stuck shut. What was with that? The voices were very close now.

"He's waking up." one of them said.

Kelly?

Sean opened his right eye and followed the voice, trying to find his friend. He was suddenly scared; he wanted to see his friend.

"Are you going to stay with us this time?" Kelly's voice was like music to Sean's ears.

Sean smiled. He could vaguely make out Kelly's features.

"How are you feeling?" Otis's voice came from somewhere behind Kelly.

"You look like crap, by the way." Randy was somewhere in the room as well.

Sean peered around the room with a broad grin on his face, trying to focus on them. Why was his face so tight? What was the deal with his left eye?

"Where am I? Why can't I open my eye?" Sean finally muttered.

"You're in the hospital," Randy responded. "Your head is covered with bandages and your eye is filled with gauze and covered by a patch. Like I said before, you look like crap."

"What happened?" Sean asked, suddenly feeling very uneasy.

"That prick Kevin Lakes cracked your skull with a beer bottle," Kelly replied.

Sean cringed. For the first time he noticed a splitting pain in his head. He noticed an older man, dressed in white, coming up behind Kelly.

"You'll be okay, son," the man commented. "It took more than 50 stitches to put you back together again. We removed some glass pieces from your eye and it's patched until the swelling goes down."

Sean's mind wandered. Did he have any place important to be today where he would look funny if he showed up looking like a mummy?

"Dino!" Sean exclaimed as he sat straight up in the bed. The excruciating pain from his side and head knocked him right back to his semi-reclined position before he could finish his sentence.

"What time is it?" Sean asked when he regained his wind. "I need to unlock the school to let Dino in to run at 6:30."

"It's close to 10:00 already," Kelly replied. "I'm sure that somebody let him in."

Sean hoped for the best, suddenly feeling very uneasy and guilty about possibly letting his team down. Would Dino make weight? Would Nick wrestle well without the right coaching support? How could he let his team suffer due to his own injury?

"I've got to get to the tournament," he stammered. "I'm coaching today."

"You're not going anywhere until at least Monday," the doctor interjected. "You have a concussion. We're not sure if it's from the bottle, the fall or multiple kicks to your head and body, but we need to keep you around for observation."

The whole scenario hurt Sean's head. He couldn't imagine letting his team down, yet he had no idea to what extent he was injured. As if reading his mind, Kelly moved close to Sean's head.

"Like I said," Kelly repeated. "Kevin Lakes busted your head with a beer bottle. Apparently, he and a couple of his buddies kicked you around when you were on the ground until that assistant coach from the university wrestling team laid Lakes out, shattering his jaw. Angie said that it was the most brutal thing she's ever seen. She called me around 2:00 a.m. after the cops stopped questioning her about what she had seen. Lakes is in a room down the hall under police surveillance for assault and battery. They took the assistant coach in on the same charges. He sounds like one mean mother."

Sean was amazed that Cole Tyler had come to his rescue. He didn't get the impression that the man cared that much for him. What would he think if it had all been for naught and Sean let his team down?

"Guys," Sean pleaded, trying to make eye contact with all three of his fraternity brothers. "I really need to get to the tournament. My team needs me."

"Sean, you need to rest," Otis interrupted.

For the comment, he received an immediate non-verbal response as Kelly smacked the young man in the back of the head. He glared at Otis as he again approached Sean's bedside.

"We'll get you there," he promised. "We won't let you down."

Chapter 67

Nick was elated to see Dino enter the South High School locker room, accompanied by Coach Granger. There was a spring in the big guy's step that made Nick feel that good news was imminent.

Joel Vassec was the first to greet the two, "Hurry up," the boy commented. "We only have five minutes until weigh-in is over. You're not fat, are you?"

"Our scale said a quarter pound under. I should be good," responded Dino, shedding his clothing and walking over to the scale where South Coach Dan Nestor and a tournament official stood waiting.

"I was almost hoping you wouldn't make it, for Joe's sake," Nestor commented, referring to South's 215-pound competitor.

Dino grinned as he stepped onto the digital scale and watched the numbers rise. His grin soon faded though as the reading stagnated at 217.2 and stopped. The tournament official eyed the boy with concern. Everyone looked at each other as Dino turned pale and donned a look of grief.

"That scale's not right," Granger commented.

"It was just calibrated yesterday," the rival coach responded. "We can try the other one if you want; it was calibrated at the same time."

Dino moved to the mechanical scale which showed the same result. The tournament official continued to increase the weight until a crack of light shown through at just under 217 and one quarter pounds.

"217 and just under a quarter," Nestor commented. "I'm sorry, Dino. I really am."

Granger pulled Nestor aside, steaming with rage.

"He made it, Nestor, I saw the scale."

"There is nothing wrong with these scales," Nestor commented. "Everyone else in the tournament has weighed in on them this morning. The seeding is done, weigh-in is done in five minutes and he can't cut a quarter pound in that time. I don't know what you want me to do."

"If he doesn't place in the conference, he doesn't go to state," Granger growled.

Both men looked at Dino. The wrestler didn't look back at them or anyone else in the room. He just looked down, appearing as if he may cry.

"Am I out of the tournament?" Dino asked softly as his coach approached him.

"No," Granger replied. "There is one other way."

Chapter 68

Nick was a bundle of nervous energy as he prepared to walk onto the mat with his team. This was the day. This was HIS day. There was no stopping him now.

The boy looked around at his team. Everyone seemed ready with the exception of the big guy in street clothes. Clifford Vassec stood beside his father, ready to cheer his team to victory after a last-minute executive decision by Coach Granger. Dino would be wrestling heavyweight in Clifford's place.

Somehow, the boys all found their places on time and stood on the mat for the playing of *The Star Spangled Banner*. Nick looked over at Dino. Despite the senior's shaky morning, he looked as solid as ever. His first match would be a substantial test for him as Dino would be wrestling the second seed, a boy to whom Dino was giving up nearly fifty pounds who had been consistently ranked in the top five in the state. Still Dino appeared unfazed, as indestructible as ever.

Nick looked to the bleachers where Ron sat, as promised, with their father. He had commented to Nick earlier that he was going to try to blend into the background and go unnoticed. Nick wondered how it would feel to be in his brother's position. Last year at this tournament, he had proven himself to be as unstoppable as Nick felt. This year, he was held captive by the physical limitations of his own body. Yet he had proven to be a man of his word and expected Nick to be the same and win the conference championship.

As the national anthem ended, Nick's attention was drawn to a large man who looked vaguely familiar. This man and another young man who appeared to have just stepped out of GQ magazine were helping a third man with a head wrapped in bandages into the gym. Nick watched the scene for several seconds before it finally dawned on him that the big guy was Coach MacCallister's roommate. Looking closer, he identified his assistant coach's jaw line, protruding below the mess of wrappings.

"You made it!" Nick exclaimed, running over to the trio. "Are you okay?"

MacCallister held his head as if the sound of a voice was too much for him. His eyes were glazed over but he gave his usual smile as Nick drew near.

"Castle, I wouldn't miss seeing you win your first championship for the world," he responded quietly, placing his hand on the boy's shoulder.

The first match was announced over the loud speaker, causing the crowd to suddenly roar. Sean cringed in agony. In his current state, it would be a long day for the young man.

"Should you be in a hospital?" Nick asked, suddenly very concerned.

"He should be," Randy replied, "but we got creative."

The young man didn't expand on what he meant by these words. There was no reason for him to mention that they had left Otis in Sean's hospital bed as a decoy, his head all wrapped in bandages in hopes that Sean would not be missed for a few hours.

* * *

The crowd roared again and Sean winced in pain. He was feeling more and more as if he had made a mistake by leaving the hospital. He had been at the tournament for several hours and his pain killers had nearly worn off.

At the same time, he was glad that he had come as he had been witness to some of the best wrestling his team had done all year. Castle, Hermanns, Vassec and Benz had all made their way through their respective matches and were awaiting their chance to step onto the mat for the semi-finals.

It did not surprise Sean that Dino had won but it did surprise him that the big guy had won convincingly against several competitors much larger than him. What concerned Sean was the sight of Dan Bota. Randy had commented that the guy was an animal as Bota tossed a 245-pound opponent around like a rag doll. He was the number one heavyweight in the state, the future heavyweight at the university and, all-in-all, 280 pounds of pure mean. Compared to Bota, Dino was a runt. Yet, if Dino won in the semi-finals, this was who he would face in the championship.

Chapter 69

Nick aggressively pushed his advantage, taking Tim Rich to the mat hard, but out of bounds. The other boy screamed in pain, causing the ref to stop the match.

"Injury time," the ref announced.

Nick watched his opponent grabbing his thumb and crouching over it as if there was something life threatening about it.

"Faker," Nick thought as he walked back to his corner. He had seen this same boy fake injuries several times in the past in order to get some rest.

Nick himself was breathing a bit heavy but not nearly the way his opponent was. Nick had dominated every facet of this match so far. With a minute and fifty three seconds left in the third period, Nick led by a score of thirteen to three. All he needed was another takedown and three back points and he would win by technical fall.

Granger greeted Nick with his usual gritty stare.

"With your head up like that you're asking to be thrown," the man commented immediately upon Nick's arrival.

Nick noticed that Sean was very slow to move from his chair to his wrestler's side.

"Should I try a fireman's carry?" Nick asked, panting slightly.

Granger shook his head.

"A double leg would be better but go with what you think will be effective," the head coach replied. Then, changing the subject, he asked, "This guy doesn't like you, does he?"

Nick pondered for a minute that Ron had beaten Tim Rich in the semi-finals a year ago in a routing very similar to this match.

"He just doesn't like the fact that he's going to lose to a Castle in the semi-finals two years in a row," Nick replied.

"Let him focus on the past," Granger instructed. "You focus on this match. You've got a nice lead."

Slow to join the conversation, Sean added his two cents, "If you can bring him to his back with the fireman's, you can get the technical fall right now."

"But if you're going to lock up with him, be careful of the throw," Granger clarified.

Nick just nodded and smiled at Sean before turning to walk back to the center of the mat. On his way, he took a moment to find Ron and his dad in the front row of the bleachers. As Ron gave him a 'thumbs up', Nick pointed to his brother in acknowledgement and smiled.

Nick stared at his opponent, not oblivious to the anger in his eyes but at the same time not concerned. He would not let down his guard. He had gotten to this point by being aggressive. Staying aggressive would be the key to winning this match, catapulting him into the finals.

As the ref blew the whistle, Nick's move was instantaneous. He shot a double leg and got his face planted in the mat for his efforts. Rotating out and losing his grip, Nick and Rich both scrambled to get their footing and face each other again.

On the attack again, Nick pressed his opponent as Rich retreated backward. "Was he winded?" Nick wondered as he moved to position his left arm over Rich's and set him up for a fireman's carry, his main concern being the boy's back-peddling which was bringing them close to the edge of the mat. "Why would Rich be stalling at a time like this?"

The thought was still in his mind, resonating through his temporal lobe as Nick's head and arm became trapped in Rich's grasp. An onlooker would have described the look on Nick's face as vague, confused or blank as his feet left the ground.

Reflexes took over as Nick grasped his opponent, bracing himself for the impact with the mat.

It was the outside of his right ankle that first made contact, not with the mat, but with the scorers' table at the mat's edge. It was a dull thud, followed by a screaming pain that resonated up Nick's calf, halfway to his knee. A moment later, Nick's torso was slammed to the mat with Rich landing on top of him, knocking the wind completely out of the boy.

The whistle blew as Nick struggled to stay off of his back.

"Out of bounds, no points," the ref exclaimed.

Everything seemed to be moving in slow motion as Nick rolled to his stomach, winced in pain and pushed himself up to his hands and knees.

"Shake it off," he thought. "Go to your corner and get taped."

Getting to his feet, Nick took one tender step onto his left foot. The ankle completely buckled under his weight, causing him to scream, as he collapsed to the mat in pain.

As Granger and Sean rushed to Nick, a female trainer from the other team joined them. As she touched his ankle, Nick screamed again.

"Why is this happening now?" Nick thought. "Everything is going so well. I'm NOT backing out now."

The tears were welling up in his eyes as he tried to be brave. "Just tape it up, Coach, I've got this match won."

Granger looked at the trainer who had turned a ghostly white. With a sad look in her eyes, she declared, "It's broken."

"Broken? It can't be broken," Nick thought. "I'm on a roll. I'm unbreakable."

"Coach, let me finish." Nick pleaded. "I can still wrestle."

Granger's words were distant as he answered, "Not today, Nick. Not today."

Nick turned to Sean, pleading, "Don't make me throw this match."

His assistant coach looked as bad off as the wrestler.

"You're not throwing it, kid. You're saving yourself for the future. There will be another time," Sean consoled him.

As Nick's gaze fell on Ron in the stands, a tear finally escaped and flowed down Nick's cheek. Looking back to Sean, he saw a matching tear on his assistant coach's cheek as well. Sean's eyes rolled back but luckily Granger caught him before he completely collapsed.

"Both of you need to get to the hospital," the coach commented.

As Nick watched the referee raise Rich's hand in victory, he buried his face in his hands. He had let one tear slip, but that would be it. He would not cry over this loss.

Chapter 70

Nick sat on the couch sulking. He was amazed and sickened at how he had fallen so far so fast, both literally and figuratively. His ankle throbbed and the cast around it itched. He half-wished that the doctors had cut the whole thing off. It wouldn't do him any more good this year.

The call from Oscar minutes earlier had not improved Nick's mood at all. The little guy had called to report that Rich had gone on to win the conference championship, Nick's conference championship. This news flash gave him the biggest headache as he sat moping. He couldn't believe he had walked into that throw. Nick was clearly the better wrestler and had beaten himself. How could he ever gain faith in himself if he could drop a match like that?

The unmistakable sound of Ron's wheelchair entering the room drew Nick's attention but he refused to change his focus as Nick had avoided his brother most of the day. He didn't want any lectures about how stupid he was to get caught in a head and arm throw when he had been so close to winning the match. Nor did he need a pep talk about how all would be better next season once his ankle healed, not that his older brother would ever give such a pep talk. Next season didn't matter. All that mattered was that Nick would be sidelined for his sophomore year state tournament. There was no getting that back.

Fortunately, neither a lecture nor a pep talk was what Ron had on his mind. Nick avoided Ron's eyes as his brother gave the update. "Bradford called, Joel took second. Your buddy Dino is probably on the mat right now wrestling Bota."

The news only marginally improved Nick's mood. He wished that he could be in the gym, supporting Dino in this match. Nick always thought of Dino as 'the big man' but he would be dwarfed by Bota, the state's top heavyweight. The mountain of a kid outweighed Dino by nearly 70 pounds and often won matches by falling on people. Of course, there had to be more to his repertoire than just falling as he sported an undefeated record this season.

Nick turned his face completely away from his brother, pretending to try to sleep. He wondered whether or not Dino would be invited to the state tournament as a heavyweight if he only placed second in the conference tournament. He was surprised to feel something move on the couch behind him. Annoyed, he looked over his shoulder to see what his brother was up to.

"I'm glad we're on equal footing again. This allows me to kick your butt," Ron joked wryly.

He had taken Nick's crutches from the couch and, using one as a sword, he poked his little brother in the lower back.

"Give them back!" Nick commanded.

Nick could hardly believe that Ron was bothering him on this, the darkest of evenings. Nick had never bothered Ron by taking his wheelchair. Why did his older brother have to pick tonight to torment him?

"Nope, I need them," the reply came.

"You're going to need them to protect your head in a minute if you don't give them back."

Ron ignored his brother's threat as he pushed his chair backward, using the crutches as poles. That having been done, he locked the wheels on his wheelchair and moved the footrest to free his legs. He then planted the stops of the crutches on the hard wood floor, lunged forward and stood upright in front of his brother for the first time in nearly a year. Nick was shocked.

Ron imitated a TV reporter's voice as he announced, "Riverside wrestler Ron Castle has sustained a spinal cord injury and will not walk again…"

He hobbled forward, taking one very tentative step, then a second with the crutches and Ron's upper body doing the majority of the work. He changed back to his own voice to finish the commentary, "…my butt."

Nick watched in awe as Ron made several more painful steps and ended his journey by slowly lowering himself into the chair adjacent to Nick's couch. The younger boy took several moments to put together a coherent question.

"How long have you been able to do this?"

"About a week," Ron replied. "I was working up to walking to the mat after you won the conference title but you didn't quite do your part."

The last sentence drew Nick's focus back to where it had been at the start of the conversation.

"Thanks for reminding me," the boy said sullenly.

"Hey, quit your whining. You miss one tournament, I missed the entire season."

The phone on the table between them rang and Ron's reflexes proved to be faster as both boys lunged to pick it up.

Nick waited impatiently as his brother really got into the call throwing out an occasional, "Really?" and "No way," but nothing that Nick could piece into a story.

It seemed like forever to Nick as he waited for his brother to hang up the phone. When he did, Ron was all smiles as he reported that, not only had Dino won the championship match three points to one, Bota had thrown such a fit afterward that he had been disqualified and would not be competing in the state tournament at all.

Nick had to smile at the news. While this had been an awful day for him on the mat, he had gotten to witness the rebirth of his brother's legs and the announcement that Dino was going to state as a heavyweight. With Bota out of the picture, Nick doubted that anyone could top Riverside's indestructible big man. Surely earning a state title would make him a sought-after commodity with university recruiters.

Life was good for his brother and life was very good for Benzy, Nick thought. For the first time in several hours, he allowed himself to smile.

Chapter 71

What was that ringing? Nick pulled the pillow over his head, trying to make it stop. Everything was dark as he slowly woke from his sleep. He heard a click and then his father's voice.

"Do you know what time it is?"

Nick didn't know what time it was. He only knew that his entire room was pitch black so it couldn't be time to get up. His ankle throbbed. He quietly cursed the person for waking him up to feel the pain.

"Oh my God!"

His dad's voice sounded more surprised than angry. Nick had assumed that it must be a prank caller at this hour, now he wasn't sure. He said a quick prayer, asking for his grandparents to be all right and then struggled to position himself to see the clock without aggravating his ankle.

Nick listened intently, waiting for some other clues from his father. The clock read 5:40.

"He'll be there. They both will."

"Who would be calling at this hour?" Nick wondered. "Was it the newspaper? They couldn't expect him to deliver papers in his condition, could they?" He thought they had gotten that all worked out the prior night.

There were footsteps in the hall and Nick's door opened.

"Dad, was it the paper?" Nick asked. "They said that someone would cover my route."

"No, Nick," his father replied.

Even in the dim light, Nick could tell that his father was shaken up.

"It was Coach Granger. He wants you to come into practice."

"I can't…"

Mr. Castle interrupted his son. "He doesn't expect you to practice. Dino got hurt last night. He just wants the team there at 7:00. You get dressed. I'm going to wake your brother."

As his father closed the door and left, Nick lay in bed, utterly confused. Vassec hadn't said anything about Dino getting hurt.

Maybe Dino's injuries were similar to Nick's and that is why the coach wanted him there?

If his presence could help Dino, Nick wouldn't protest. He moved as quickly as his ankle would allow and got ready to go.

* * *

Nick was tense as he hobbled toward the gym. His dad was somewhere behind him, pushing Ron. Nick needed to get to the gym NOW to find out what was going on. All his dad had been able to tell him in the car was that Dino had been in a fight and gotten hurt.

Nick hoped that he could be of some help. Dino's last shot at a state title was the following weekend. Nick needed to see his friend to know that he wouldn't let an injury stop him the way Nick had. Benzy wouldn't let anything get in his way. One of them had to be the best this year.

Coming around the corner into the gym, he noticed that nearly the entire team was assembled although Dino was strangely absent. Coach Granger was walking slowly to the group with his arm around Oscar who was a pasty white and looked like he hadn't slept. What was going on?

"Sit down, boys," Granger started. "We won't be practicing today. Mr. Benz asked that we all gather. He'll be here shortly. In the meantime, Oscar will tell you what he knows."

All eyes turned intently to the one person on the team whose words never held any weight. The small boy stammered as he told his story.

"Benzy's dad drove us to A'Romano's last night because Dino wanted to talk with Cheri Winters and show her his championship plaque. He was all excited too because some university recruiters had waited around for him after the championship match and had verbally offered him scholarships. He really wanted to let Cheri know."

"Good old Benzy," Nick thought. "He never misses a chance to try to impress Cheri." He looked around to see if Dino had arrived yet. He still needed to congratulate the big guy on his big match from the prior night.

"Dino's dad waited in the car and Dino went into the bathroom right away because there was this lady ahead of us. This big guy came in behind me, pulled out a knife, grabbed Cheri and started yelling at her to give him the cash. Dino sneaked up on the guy and grabbed him but the guy stabbed him a couple of times before Mr. Benz came running in and bashed the guy in the head."

"Stabbed him? No, that can't be right," Nick thought.

The tears streaming down Oscar's cheeks as he uttered those words finally got the point across to Nick that something was gravely wrong.

Nick noticed that Oscar was no longer looking at the team; his eyes were affixed on something behind them. Turning around, he noticed the large frame of Dino's father, stepping quietly across the dimly lit floor. Mr. Benz was a large, solid man, approximately 6'2" and 250 pounds wearing a stained jacket and jeans. While Nick had always seen him as jovial in the past, today he looked more pale and sickly than Oscar.

"I should be at the hospital, with my family," the big man stated, his eyes searching for something in the distance. "But I know that this team has been like Dean's second family. You're the ones that he has spent his afternoons, weekends and many evenings with as long as I can remember."

Staring at Mr. Benz, it finally occurred to Nick that the stains on the man's jacket were from his son's blood.

"My son…" Mr. Benz took a deep breath as the team awaited his update.

"My son…died this morning at 3:43. He would have wanted you to hear the news from me. He was your friend. He was my hero."

Nick stared in disbelief as tears filled his eyes. The one friend who had guided him and not let him be a victim of himself, the indestructible being who never backed down from anyone was now gone. Nick buried his head in his stocking cap and let his emotions flow. He bawled like a baby and didn't care what those around him thought.

Chapter 72

Nick heard the chair move and, out of the corner of his eye, saw Coach Granger leave his seat. The boy's stomach tied itself in a double knot as he glanced toward the podium.

The moment of truth was here, or would be soon. He felt sick. He just wanted to get up and hobble away but of course he stayed, anticipating the coach's speech, both longing for and dreading the possibility of being named Summer Captain.

The vote had taken place over a week earlier as the team had gathered to cast ballots for all of the team's annual awards. He didn't think twice as Granger handed him the sheet of paper. He voted for Dino for Hardest Worker, the Spirit Award and Outstanding Wrestler. It was the least he could do to recognize the contributions of the person who had meant so much to him.

However, he had to pause before he voted for Summer Captain. His upbringing argued, "If you vote for yourself, it means you have a big ego," but they were overpowered by Dino's words echoing in his mind, "If you don't believe in yourself, you're not going to win." He would not argue with the spirit of his friend and quickly wrote "Nick Castle" on the line provided.

Now, as he sat waiting, the doubts were coming over him. Could he lead this team? Would people actually follow him? Why would they? To make matters worse, if he won, he would have to give a speech. The thought of addressing this group was more terrifying than decapitation. He couldn't even imagine what he might possibly say. Was looking stupid any way to start a career as a leader? He just wanted to go away.

Granger made his way to the microphone, looking as unkempt and grouchy as ever. "I'll keep this short in case any of you want to go back to the buffet line. Quite frankly, I'm tired of looking at your mangy mugs and am anxious to get through this."

Nick took a deep breath as the coach continued. "This is actually going to be a very short awards presentation. A single athlete was voted as winner of all of three awards. This young man exuded the work ethic to win Hardest Worker, the enthusiasm to win the Spirit Award and the drive and ability to be named this year's Outstanding Wrestler. Not surprisingly, the first person to win all three of these awards in a single season is Mr. Dino Benz."

Despite his crutches, Nick was one of the first to his feet as the wrestlers gave a standing ovation to their fallen friend as Mr. Benz approached the podium to accept his son's award. The team fell silent as the man reached the podium and collected all three trophies.

"I know Dean wasn't one to do a lot of talking in public, he was a lot like his father in that way. He let his performance do most of the talking for him. I don't know exactly what he would have said but I thought it likely that he would quote from this poem that we found in his locker. He wrote it for a class."

He runs and runs, through the night.
He stumbles many times.
It is not only the course he sees before him that keeps him at this pace.
If not in this contest, in another, he will win the race.

The room was silent as they listened to Dino's words. The poem was fitting as the big guy had excelled in so many things and never gave up when he stumbled in many others. It was a poem that any one of them could have written. Yet they captured Dino's spirit so well. He never won his state championship, but nobody who knew him could possibly argue that Dino wasn't the best 215-pound wrestler, or heavyweight for that matter, in the state.

"I know Dean is in heaven," Mr. Benz continued. "I also know that, even though it wasn't the 215-pound state championship, the race he won was one that he took pride in. Thank you."

As Mr. Benz held his son's three trophies up for everyone to see, he received a second standing ovation from the room. He passed his place on the podium over to Sean who gave him an understanding pat on the back.

Nick could not help but feel that Coach MacCallister looked older. He was wearing a suit and his left eye still had blood marks which would take several more weeks to diminish. The lasting memento from his ordeal at The Rock was a large scar that stretched across the left side of his face.

"Let me start by saying that I am glad, for your sakes, that you don't have to weigh in again until November because I saw the way you hit that buffet. After that performance, Oscar will be lucky to make weight at 215."

The room granted the young man a small chuckle.

"It was a year of changes and challenges for all of us. My job here this afternoon is to give the final award for the two young men who will carry the team through the summer and ensure that we, as a team, come back stronger next year. The first of our two Summer Captains should be no surprise. He was our highest state placer this season with his third place finish. He was a scrapper and a leader for us this year. Congratulations, Kevin Hermanns."

Nick's butterflies momentarily subsided as he watched the 145-pound wrestler walk quickly to the stage, shake Coach MacCallister's hand, accept the certificate and confidently grab the microphone.

"You had better be ready to work hard this off-season," Kevin asserted. "That is all I have to say."

There were cheers and howls as Hermanns left the stage. Nick's stomach immediately tensed up again as Sean returned to the microphone.

"The second Summer Captain was a bit more of a surprise, although he probably shouldn't have been. Even Joel Vassec led a secret campaign the day of the voting to help this wrestler take his place as Summer Captain."

"Vassec?" Nick thought. Obviously Nick hadn't won if the person about to be named had Joel's backing.

"This is an honor that the team places on a person whom they consider a leader," Sean continued. "I know there was a point this past season in which this fine young man was not considered such. In fact, there was a point when he wasn't even a member of the varsity team. However, if adversity gives strength, this wrestler will be bench pressing 1,000 pounds soon. He took each challenge handed to him, knocked it down and asked for a bigger challenge. I am proud to deliver this award to the wrestler that Granger claims is the first sophomore to ever be awarded a position as Summer Captain, Nick Castle."

The room broke into applause in unison with Nick's heart jumping into his throat. He couldn't imagine that Joel Vassec would support him in any way, yet it was his name that Coach MacCallister had announced.

Nick hobbled up to the stage, wishing that he didn't have the extra hassle of crutches to contend with. His nerves were enough of an impediment; he didn't need these extra clumsy walking devices to contribute to the picture.

Upon reaching Coach MacCallister, Nick grabbed his certificate, shook the assistant coach's hand and tried to leave but was stopped by the other wrestlers yelling, "Speech, speech!"

His greatest dream and worst nightmare had just collided. What could he possibly say? He felt himself turn red as he stumbled toward the microphone.

"Thank you," Nick mumbled, then turned to leave the podium.

A deep feeling of regret immediately seized the boy and stopped him in his tracks. How could he have come this far just to spit two words into a microphone and leave? Nick was suddenly angry with himself as he turned back to the podium to rectify the situation.

Ignoring the microphone, Nick began again, projecting his voice for the whole room to hear. "Thank you, all of you who trusted in me enough to vote for me. I won't let you down. I learned a lot this year that I didn't expect to learn. Ron taught me that, even if things look impossible, they are not. I learned from Coach MacCallister that sometimes not realizing that something can't be done is the best way to ensure that it can be done. And Dino," Nick paused to look at the ceiling. "Dino taught me that hard work doesn't get you anywhere unless you believe that it can and make it take you where you want to be. I appreciate that Dino and all of you made me look at myself and believe in my abilities.

"My brother's philosophy has always been that great wrestlers are made between November and February...but champions are made between March and October. I am honored to help Kevin lead this March to October charge."

Oscar started cheering, giving Nick a chance to calm his nerves and stay for another minute to finish what he really needed to say.

"Next year at this time, mark my words, there will be a state championship plaque resting on the mantle at the Castle house. I'm willing to do whatever it takes to be the best. I want every wrestler in this room to be at the top of that podium at the end of next season."

He hoped that nobody could see him trembling as he stepped away from the podium. He was completely dumbfounded as everyone got to their feet to give him a standing ovation. He blushed many shades of red as he made his way back to his seat.

Had he really said that? Did he just promise a state championship? Multiple state championships?

Why would he say words like that? And why was there no doubt in his mind that he would deliver?

Nick's smile glowed brighter than his blushing red cheeks as he hobbled back to his seat under the watchful eyes of a team that believed in him.

Epilogue

…three …four. Ron grabbed onto the kitchen table, transferring the weight of his entire body to his arms. He panted happily as he looked back in wonder, amazed that he had just walked four entire steps without the assistance of a walker or crutches.

The boy steadied himself and turned around so that he was half-seated on the table while continuing to let his arms bare the brunt of his weight. His walker was still standing beside the door which led to the living room. He stared at the piece of metal with grim determination. He would not need the device for much longer at the rate he was going. Yet he needed to find the strength to get to it sometime before Nick and his parents got home from the wrestling banquet. They would be livid if they knew what he had just attempted and accomplished. All three were always after him to take his rehabilitation slowly and avoid risk of injury. For Ron, it was not the way to recover.

Realizing that they could arrive home at any moment, he once again righted himself and forced his legs to support his body's weight. It was only four steps back to the walker. He would make the trip or die trying. One…

* * *

Nick hobbled briskly along the snowy sidewalk. Even the ice didn't slow him down as he kept his crutches beneath him.

This had been a day he would long remember. He estimated that most of his teammates were probably sitting at home, letting the banquet's food digest and dreaming of next season.

For Nick, next season started today. He hobbled up the steps and into the gym to work out, continuing his quest to be the best.

Breinigsville, PA USA
02 April 2010
235425BV00001B/4/P